"Hello there," Melanie whispered, slipping between the silky sheets

"Mmm."

"Are you awake?" She stroked the length of his naked back, following the bumps of his spine, his sexy tush—

He started. "Whah th—"

"Shh. It's Melanie, you dope."

"Melanie." His hoarse whisper nearly made her giggle. Poor guy must have been in a deep sleep. "What— How—"

"Don't talk, just lie back...and enjoy." She planted kisses, collarbone to throat, throat to chin, searching for that sexy mouth.

Found it. She lingered. Suddenly strong arms came around her and he was on top so fast she barely had time to react.

"Melanie." The whisper again, this time softer, sweeter, more tender. Something wasn't right.

His lips found hers dead on target, as if he could see in the dark. She lay still from shock— the man could kiss.

But it wasn't just his technique, the kissing was... different somehow.

As if he *loved* her.

Blaze

Dear Reader,

Edgar is my first nerd hero ever, and though the story sounded great while I was writing the synopsis, when it came to writing Edgar's scenes, I wasn't so sure. Was this man attractive enough to interest Melanie? Frankly, at first he wasn't even attractive enough to interest me!

But as the book progressed, I found myself getting a little weak-kneed over him, right along with Melanie, and when I wrote the last chapter, I realized I was crazy about him. As much as I love the suave alpha man, I might just have to write more heroes like Edgar.

What do you think? Enjoy a good geek once in a while? Drop me an e-mail through my Web site, www.IsabelSharpe.com, and let me know!

Cheers,

Isabel Sharpe

Isabel Sharpe

SURPRISE ME...

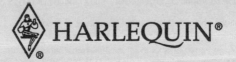

HARLEQUIN®

TORONTO • NEW YORK • LONDON
AMSTERDAM • PARIS • SYDNEY • HAMBURG
STOCKHOLM • ATHENS • TOKYO • MILAN • MADRID
PRAGUE • WARSAW • BUDAPEST • AUCKLAND

Recycling programs
for this product may
not exist in your area.

ISBN-13: 978-0-373-79543-7

SURPRISE ME...

Copyright © 2010 by Muna Shehadi Sill

www.eHarlequin.com

Printed in U.S.A.

ABOUT THE AUTHOR

Isabel Sharpe was not born pen in hand like so many of her fellow writers. After she quit work to stay home with her first born son and nearly went out of her mind, she started writing. After more than twenty novels for Harlequin—along with another son—Isabel is more than happy with her choice these days. She loves hearing from readers. Write to her at www.IsabelSharpe.com.

Books by Isabel Sharpe

HARLEQUIN BLAZE

*Men to Do
**Do Not Disturb
†The Wrong Bed
††The Martini Dares
‡Forbidden Fantasies
‡‡The Wrong Bed: Again and Again

Don't miss any of our special offers. Write to us at the following address for information on our newest releases.

Harlequin Reader Service
U.S.: 3010 Walden Ave., P.O. Box 1325, Buffalo, NY 14200
Canadian: P.O. Box 609, Fort Erie, Ont. L2A 5X3

To Joe Biebel,
who helped me learn about fencing,
and who I bet has never been mentioned in a
romance novel before

1

"So…?"

Melanie Hawthorne took a leisurely sip of her mojito, served with a stick of Hawaiian sugar cane at her favorite after-work hot spot, The Wicked Hop, and carefully put the glass back down on the bar. She knew exactly what Jenny was asking, but she was going to enjoy this to its fullest. "I'm sorry, so…what?"

Jenny accepted her drink from the friendly blond bartender they liked to flirt with. Usually she was surreptitiously checking out the scene, but right now she was 100 percent fixed on Melanie. "So…have you seen Stoner since that night in Edgar's apartment?"

"Nope. I did mention I hang here after work a lot. So maybe he'll show. I know last night he had a rehearsal with his band." Just the thought that Stoner might seek her out, that they might start something hot, launched that familiar internal flutter. She loved men, bad boys in particular. And she meant *bad*. Arrogant jerks, selfish users, whatever label you came up with, Melanie homed in on them with unerring precision. She'd love to change, heck, she'd tried to change, tried to convince herself she could date a sweet, steady guy, like her best friend and co-worker, Edgar Raymond. Last week, though, she'd been in the act of suggesting that exact solution on Edgar's couch when his so-hot older brother, Stoner, had walked into the apartment. Melanie had fallen, boom, and that was that. New guy. Same old story.

"He sounds so-o-o dreamy, I can't wait to see him." Jenny sighed. "You always land these *incredible* men. I mean I'm still happy with Noah after three years, but believe me, I don't mind living vicariously."

Yeah, incredible men. For the few hours or days or even weeks of blissful fun until they invariably moved on to the next pretty face, leaving her to grieve her latest disaster until against all odds—and common sense—her natural optimism resurfaced. Melanie had the hunt/capture/lose-the-prey-again sequence down to a science—a science she, after all her rejections and failures, hoped would someday land her the mother lode, the Real Thing, True Love, a guy-to-call-her-own for more than a few sweaty, athletic hours or days or weeks. "Just call me Lucky Mel."

"Ooh, is that him?" Jenny's brown eyes had about tripled in size. She brushed her black, slanted bangs out of the way and stared toward the entrance, craning her neck to see through the crowd. "Tall, dark hair, bodacious bod."

Melanie tried to turn around casually, but turning around casually was pretty hard to do moving as fast as possible. She scanned the bodies by the front door and shook her head. "I don't see him."

"Aw." Jenny sucked down more mojito to cushion the disappointment. "So he's a rock star, huh?"

"He plays in a band. 'Imploding Bovines.'"

"Imploding...ew, really?"

"Some statement about the world economy and the beef industry and the environment...I don't know." Melanie shrugged, wishing she was sitting where Jenny was so she could monitor the entrance. "Edgar was kind of rolling his eyes when he told me. I don't think he and his brother get along too well."

"Well, if Stoner looks and acts anything like you say, they sound like exact opposites."

"I guess." She took another sip of her mojito, noting that the drink was half-gone; she'd better slow down. Edgar was... Edgar. Big nose, horrible hair, ghastly fashion sense, but great teeth and a fabulous smile, gorgeous blue eyes—the nicest man in the world. Of course, him being a great catch in all the ways that mattered, Melanie felt only sisterly affection no matter how hard she tried. God forbid she fall for a man who would treat her well.

"Omigod. That's *got* to be Stoner." Jenny clutched Melanie's arm and pointed. "There. Beside the tall guy with the red shirt. All in black. Wow, you totally weren't kidding. Those blue eyes are amazing. I can feel the heat from here!"

Melanie turned, adrenaline burning from chest to toes. Stoner shared those blue eyes with Edgar, but while Edgar's eyes were warm with shy friendliness, Stoner's blazed with sexual mischief which made Melanie weak in the... everything.

Like the first time she saw him, he wore black. Black tight T-shirt and black jeans with a silver-studded belt. Black hair, not quite as thick and curled as Edgar's, in a tousled I-don't-care style that probably took him hours. "That's him."

Stoner scanned the bar coolly until his eyes lit on Melanie's, and his sex appeal shot across the room as if he'd cast a hook. She was hit. All he had to do was reel her in.

He swaggered over, and while the crowd didn't really part to let him through, it almost seemed that way to Melanie because she couldn't believe the male power he had, and she couldn't stop staring.

"Hey there, Mel-a-nie." He kissed her cheek; his warm lips lingered, making her shiver. "How ya doing?"

"Great, now that you're here." She looked him straight

in the eyes, buzzing full throttle from the mojito and his presence.

"Good to hear." He winked and cocked his head toward Jenny. "And who's *this?*"

Jenny nearly slid to the floor in her eagerness. "Jenny Tremont. I work with Melanie. We're *so* going to come hear your band!"

Melanie kept herself from rolling her eyes. *So going to come hear your band?* Jenny was twenty-nine, but sometimes managed to sound like a tweenager groupie. "You're playing at Bad Genie Rock Lounge this week, right?"

"You remembered." He lifted his chin toward the bartender, who came over as if he'd been waiting all night for his chance to serve this drink. "I'll have a Leinie's Red and whatever these ladies are having, another round for them."

"Ooh, thanks, Stoner." Jenny batted her black-lined eyes at him. "I'll be loose and easy after two of these."

"Yeah?" He grinned a predator's grin, which probably made all the women in visual range immediately wish they were prey. "How about you, Mel? Your barriers go down after a little alcoholic lube job?"

Melanie wasn't an English major, but she thought that metaphor was pretty mixed up. However, substandard grammar was not going to stand between her and a chance for fun time with Stoner.

"Barriers?" She arched on the stool, tilted her head. "What barriers?"

His laugh was low and rich, so much like Edgar's it startled her. Their voices were eerily similar, too. If she turned around when he was talking she might get them confused. But that was about the only way to mistake one for the other, and she saw no reason to turn her back to Stoner...until later, maybe. "You are my kind of girl, Mel-a-nie."

"Mmm, no." She waggled her finger at him, loving the way he leisurely half sang her name. "I'm all woman."

"I stand corrected." He took his beer, clinked it with her glass, then Jenny's, then with hers again. His eyes skittered over her body and landed on her mouth with intensity that made her feel already kissed. "Yeah, you are *all* woman."

Melanie tossed her hair and pouted to suck the straw of her drink, making sure he was watching. The familiar sex-machinery inside her hummed steadily now. This was going to be one excellent evening. Instinct told her so, and her instinct when it came to men and sex was never, ever wrong. Stoner would be a passionate, selfish lover, slightly rough, mostly un-schooled, a lover who assumed his own amazing-ness would turn her on so terrifically that he didn't need to do much more than just be him. Gymnastic, inventive, a show-off, he'd use many rooms and many positions.

Bring it on.

There was nothing like that first time, when she could be a man's perfect fantasy woman. Nothing like the erotic excitement of new bodies discovering each other, finding ways to please—light, lovely, no baggage, no boredom, no boundaries.

"So you're Edgar's brother." Jenny took her sugar cane stick out of her drink and bit down, sucking out the sweet syrup.

"Yup." He drained half his beer as if it were lemonade.

"You don't seem much alike."

"Never have been."

"Even as kids?" Melanie asked.

"Not even. I was into everything, and he was scared of everything. Bugs, worms, even the swing." He laughed. "I'd push him like a few inches on that thing, and he'd scre-e-eam."

Melanie immediately felt protective of poor baby Edgar. "I was scared of bugs, too, as a kid. And thunder. Still am, though not as much."

"Yeah?" He grinned his sexy grin again. "If it storms while I'm in town, you run to me, baby."

"I will." She let her eyes smolder at him. "Maybe even if it doesn't storm."

"Whoa." He rocked back on his heels, chuckling. "I'd take you up on that in a heartbeat, Mel-a-nie."

"You may have to." She licked her lips sensually.

Jenny muttered something else under her breath, nearly making Melanie giggle in the midst of her sex-goddess act. "Luckily, Edgar grew up braver than that."

"Seriously. And he is one smart dude." Stoner nodded slowly. "Smart plus classy. Like my parents."

"You come from class?" Jenny sounded so surprised that, thank goodness, Stoner cracked up instead of being insulted. Point in his favor, he could laugh at himself. "I mean, I didn't mean—"

"Nah, it's okay. Go figure, huh? I never fit into that country club shi—stuff, sorry, ladies."

"Country club?" Melanie was astounded. Edgar? How could she not know that about him?

"I was a rebel from the beginning. Gave my parents hell."

"Ha." Another reason Melanie loved bad boys. She understood them. "I was like that, too."

"Yeah?" He moved closer, his hip touching her thigh, bared by her short clingy black skirt. "A wild one, huh?"

"My poor grandparents haven't recovered yet. They had to move to Florida to get away from me."

"Aw, c'mon."

She giggled, nearly emptying her mojito. "Maybe not only to get away from me."

"What about parents?"

"Mom was even wilder than me. She wasn't around much, and when she was, there were different men in and out all the time."

"In and out, huh?" He rotated his hip back and forth against her thigh. "Tell me more about that concept."

She would, but her mind had turned to lust-mush. "Maybe later?"

"Definitely later."

"Her mom just came back to town." Jenny finished her mojito and picked up the one Stoner had bought her. "She's trying to settle down and change her ways."

"Aw, man." Stoner shook his head sorrowfully. "You can't fight who you are. There's no point. Like I said, I knew early on I was different from my family. There was nothing I could do about it but be me. So that's who I am."

Melanie wanted to applaud. "I totally agree with you."

"Well, then, cheers, girl—sorry. Ms. Mel-a-nie, she is *a-all* woman." He clinked their glasses, drained his beer and thunked it on the bar. "And I am sad to say, I gotta get going."

Melanie's adrenaline petered out abruptly.

"Already?" Jenny looked as bewildered as Melanie felt.

"I have somewhere to be tonight. I just stopped by to see if I could catch you." He slid his arm around Melanie's shoulder. "Bang, you're caught."

Melanie tipped back to look directly into his bottomless blue pools of sex. "I know."

"I should be home to Edgar's place by midnight." He glanced carelessly around the bar, then angled his head lazily back toward hers. "I'm heading *right* to bed."

Her petered-out adrenaline came flooding back. "Really…"

"I hear Edgar doesn't lock his apartment at night." His voice had dropped, for her ears only. She was getting every word. "Or at least he's going to forget tonight."

She pretended to look shocked. "How careless."

"And guess what." He leaned forward until his lips touched her cheek. "Edgar is such a good guy that he's given up his bedroom for me so I can sleep in when he has to get up for work."

"Is that so?" She could barely get sound out, battered by a surge of hormones broadcasting their readiness for this man. Tonight. After midnight. In Edgar's—

Edgar's bed? With Edgar in the apartment? *Oh, no.* She couldn't—

"It's a nice big bed. Clean sheets." His voice rumbled through her, his lips brushed her cheek at every syllable. "Very comfortable."

"Your brother..."

"Won't be home. He's visiting a friend in...Chicago. Last-minute thing."

Melanie frowned. Edgar hadn't told her that. Though, if he wasn't going to be home...

"Well." She turned. Stoner's lips touched the corner of her mouth. "That might change things."

"I hope it does." He lingered a blissful second, then drew back and took her hand for a formal shake. "Very nice to see you, Ms. Mel-a-nie."

"And you, Mr. Stoner."

"I hope to see you again—" he brought her hand to his mouth for a gallant kiss "—very soon."

"We'll see." She kept her cool, all the while dying to jump down from her stool and go skipping around the bar shrieking *yes, yes, yes!*

Nothing in this world, *nothing,* fired her up like a sexy guy wanting her. The pumped-up thrill took over her, made the world a fabulous place bursting with possibilities.

Stoner said goodbye to Jenny, left one last piercing blue look with Melanie and exited the bar, probably sure they were staring at his fabulous shoulders and ass disappearing into the crowd, which they both were.

"What did he say? What's going on? Are you going to meet him later?"

Melanie smiled dreamily. Why fight it? She knew inviting random encounters was a bad way to live, knew it was a crazy way to look for love, knew men who approached her like this were not in the mood for any kind of real relationship, but heck, she couldn't resist. She had her mother's genes. And look at Mom—fifty-one and only recently deciding it was time to renounce her self-indulgent lifestyle.

Which meant Melanie had another twenty-five years of fabulous high after fabulous high to look forward to. Starting tonight, with the current man of her dreams, through an unlocked apartment door into a nice-size room holding a big, clean and ready-for-action bed.

MELANIE STRODE DOWN Water Street in the cool night air, checking her watch by the nearest streetlight even knowing it would be exactly one minute later than the last time she checked it. Which put her at forty-five minutes past midnight, enough time, she hoped, for Stoner to have made it back from wherever he'd gone, gotten into bed as promised, and to have given up on her and fallen asleep.

After Stoner left, she'd had another mojito with Jenny at The Wicked Hop, then they'd gone to hear a band at the Milwaukee Ale House, where she drank a lot of water and nursed a beer for appearances, not wanting to show up in Stoner's bed too drunk to function. Before it was time to leave, though, she'd poured back one last mojito to make sure any inhibitions—she didn't have many—would be on hold.

So now, well-hydrated, high on adrenaline and that last quickly downed drink, she was on her way.

To Stoner. *Oh, yeah.*

At the entrance to Edgar's funny little building, she pushed through the outer door…then stopped. *Oh, no.* Stoner might have made sure the door to Edgar's apartment would be open, but the inner door to the building was locked. She'd have to buzz him to let her in, which wasn't the end of the world, but announcing herself would spoil the fun of creeping into the bedroom and jumping him in the dark. Not that he'd be totally surprised, but she never had actually told him whether she'd show, so she had a shot at a stealth attack.

Maybe someone would come out? Thursday night, it could happen this late. She peered through the glass, hand next to her face to block the light from the foyer. The last several steps of the staircase were visible…and empty.

Three impatient, fidgety minutes later, they were still empty, but the now familiar row of buzzers next to the door gave her another idea. Sledge, the artist/sculptor/jeweler, lived in Edgar's building on the second floor, the guy she'd met when Edgar took her to buy a necklace for his longtime "girlfriend," who turned out, incredibly, not to exist.

Melanie frowned, boozily distracted by a new thought. What had happened to that necklace if there was no girlfriend to give it to? Maybe the whole scene had been a charade and Edgar hadn't really bought it. Except that made no sense either because—

Focus, Melanie. The *point* was that she could buzz Sledge and say she needed to get into Edgar's apartment, that she was early for a rendezvous and wanted to wait until he got back from…somewhere. With luck, Sledge wouldn't know Edgar had gone to Chicago.

Good plan. Except it was rudely late to be bothering anyone.

She was reaching for Sledge's buzzer anyway when jeans appeared on the stairs inside the building, and then rapidly, the rest of a young guy. *Perfect.*

"Hey there." He held the door open for her with a friendly smile. "Forget your key?"

"Visiting a friend in 3C."

"Excellent. Have a good night."

"Thanks!" Oh, she *so* would, partly because of him.

Inside, she hauled a mirror out of her bag for one last check, even though she'd already primped in the ladies' room at the Milwaukee Ale House. Lipstick—check; eyelashes darkened and curled—check; blush not too garish—check; hair appropriately mussed—check; clothes...

Melanie interrupted her routine. A sudden vision appeared, of her mother preparing for a night out with whatever man she was seeing that week or month, exactly like this, checking lips, eyes, cheeks, hair...with Melanie as a little girl watching, torn between admiration for her mom's beauty, envy at the way she got to fancy herself up, and anxiety, not knowing if the date would last all evening, all night or all week, leaving her and Alana to fend for themselves.

Funny she'd never noticed the similarity of their preparation before, though of course she realized she was like her mom in a lot of other ways, ahem. The association probably occurred to her now because Mom had come back to Milwaukee, apparently hoping to repair the damage she'd done to the relationship with her daughters.

Melanie shoved the mirror into her purse, unwilling to continue even if the connection to her mother was only superficial. Melanie didn't have kids she was leaving alone and scared tonight. She was the only one who'd shoulder any consequences for her actions.

She started up the stairs, not wanting to dwell on negative thoughts. Tonight was a mission of pure fun.

Up one flight, turn at the landing, up another to the second floor where Sledge lived—she tiptoed past his door—up another, turn at the landing, up again to floor three, apartment C, the door that was supposed to be unlocked.

Yes. She turned the knob silently, took a deep breath, body thrumming with excitement, and slipped into the dark interior. She'd known Edgar two years but had only seen his place for the first time last week, and had been shocked. From the mismatched, horrible way Edgar dressed, she'd expected his apartment to be a typical bachelor disaster.

Nope.

The place was nothing like him—or nothing like the

way she thought of him. Sophisticated, stylish, elegant even, cherry-toned woods and green plants and a colorful—and very clean—fish tank, state-of-the-art kitchen, impressive library... Add that to Stoner's revelation of a country-club upbringing and it didn't equal the dorky, disorganized friend Melanie thought she knew.

She moved into the living room, eerily lit by the glowing light above the bubbling tank. Straight ahead to the right, a door, ajar as Stoner said it would be. Melanie headed for it, walking silently, hoping he was asleep. She wanted to slide into bed, wake him gently with kisses and caresses, get their intimacy off to a slow, tantalizing start.

Through the door, and into...

The bathroom. Arghh.

She made a quick exit and tiptoed down the hall a few feet to the next door. Also ajar. She pushed it open halfway, pleased when it didn't protest.

Very dark inside, only the faintest glimmer around the blinds. A body barely visible in the bed, the sound of deep, regular breathing.

Hello, Melanie. Welcome to your perfect fantasy. We hope you enjoy your stay.

Oh, she was pretty sure she would.

As quietly as she could, she laid her purse on the floor, then took hold of the hem of her top and pulled it off slowly, as if she were stripping with Stoner watching. She imagined his reaction, her heightened sensual awareness reveling in the feel of the room's cool air on her skin. *Yes, oh, yes; he liked that, but wanted to see more.* Bra unhooked, she let it fall, watching the lump on the bed, imagining his eyes glazing, hands reaching for her.

Skirt next, pulled off in a slow shimmy, then underpants, sliding over hips, gliding down thighs, dropping past calves to her feet, then kicked away.

Naked. Ready.

No, not yet. Condoms in her purse—*always have them, always use them,* her mother had counseled over and over, way before Melanie and Alana knew what she was talking about.

Now. Ready.

Melanie moved, floated, wafted across the floorboards until she was next to the dark shape that would give her body so much pleasure so soon. For a minute she stood by the bed, imagining, fantasizing, until her desire rose so impatiently she could no longer wait to touch him.

As slowly and gently as possible, she slid the condom under his second pillow, then slipped into the bed, displacing the mattress and covers as imperceptibly as she could. She lay next to him and he stirred, not yet aware of what disturbed his sleep.

He would be soon.

She reached and encountered a muscular bare back, skin smooth and warm. She wanted to purr. This was going to be wonderful.

"Mmm."

Melanie smiled. "Hello there."

"Ungh." He lifted and replaced his head on the pillow, drawing up his legs.

"Are you even awake yet?" She stroked the length of his back, following the bumps of his spine, the contours of his shoulder blades, up to—

He started. "Whah th—"

"Shhh." She curled around him. "It's Melanie, you dope."

"Melanie." His hoarse whisper nearly made her giggle. Poor guy must have been in a seriously deep sleep. "What— How—"

"Don't talk, sleepy man…." She put her lips to his skin, followed the taut muscle across the top of his shoulder. Desire urged her up to straddle him. Rolling him flat on his back, she discovered he slept in the nude, and that one part of him was waking up faster than the rest. She stroked the nicely developed planes of his chest through curling hair, wishing she could see his face, but enjoying the mysterious darkness around them too much to turn on a light. "Just lie back...and enjoy."

"Oh, my—"

"Shhh." She leaned down, planted kisses collarbone to throat, throat to chin, orienting herself on the landscape of his fine physique so she wouldn't aim and miss that sexy mouth when she went for their first kiss.

Found it. She lingered, lips hovering millimeters above his, making hers tingle and tremble with anticipation. Nothing beat this moment, making him wait, making herself wait, too, her body going nuts with hormones and—

Strong arms came around her; his body heaved, and he was on top so fast she barely had time to react.

"Melanie." The whisper again, this time softer, sweeter, more tender. She suddenly felt oddly disjointed, almost panicky. Something wasn't right. Something was—

His lips found hers dead on target, as if he could see in the dark. She lay still from shock—one, two, three—then her brain registered that she was being kissed as if she were his last hope of ever being kissed again, that his lips were warm and firm and that they matched hers absolutely perfectly.

She made a tiny whimpering sound of surrender that surprised her. Her arms came up and around his neck and she hung on as if she'd otherwise drown.

The man could kiss.

But it wasn't just his technique, the kissing was...different, somehow. Nothing like she'd experienced in recent memory. It was...

It was...

It was as if he *loved* her.

Stoner was kissing her as if she was the greatest thing that had ever happened or that ever could happen to him. And she was kissing him back that way because within a very short time it seemed that had become entirely true.

He lifted off her; she protested with an inarticulate sound, feeling the loss keenly…until those magic lips began exploring, circling her breasts in a slow inward spiral, making her nearly weep with gratitude when they finally found her nipple.

His hands had started a journey of their own, covering her thighs with warm sweeps that made her lift her hips from the bed, going closer and closer to her thighs' juncture, then retreating, closer, then retreating.

She was crazy hot already for the release of his touch between her legs, and they'd barely even begun. He was nothing like she expected, not selfish, not impatient, not insensitive, absolutely the opposite of all those things.

Stoner…

Her heart started a pointless yearning; she told it to stop immediately, as she had told it so many times. This was sex with a stranger, no different than all the other sex she'd had with all the other strangers.

His fingers reached the starved place between her legs; breath hissed between her teeth. Touched, withdrew, probed farther, withdrew.

It was totally different.

She moaned as he dipped again, circled slowly, retreated, circled again, then his torso moved down and he replaced his fingers with his mouth.

Melanie lay helplessly, not sure what had happened, how she'd lost control of the show to this extent. She struggled to sit up. "You should let me… I want to …"

His turn to shush her. His strong hand planted on her sternum pushed her back down. His lips closed over her clitoris and his tongue began to play in earnest.

She gasped, lifted her head, let it drop, eyes squeezed tight, fighting the pleasure. "No. Too soon."

He showed no mercy, thrust two fingers inside her and shoved her over the edge within seconds, a deep, satisfying orgasm that went on and on until she was nearly in tears, racked by the contractions and the emotion. Too soon. She only dimly understood the certainty she felt that when they joined bodies, they would also join something much more profound. Now she wouldn't get the chance anytime soon to see if that level of intimacy could happen between them. It took her hours to recharge for orgasm number two.

"I wanted to come with you."

"You will, Melanie," he whispered. Again she had the feeling something wasn't right. An odd instinct. Disconcerting. She shouldn't have had that last drink, so she could analyze her reaction more clearly.

He stretched beside her on his side, a dark shape in the darkened room, no longer serving her but an equal partner. She slid her hand down his lean abdomen; he was hard, which pleased her. It meant the work of making her come hadn't been work.

A sweep down his granite length with an open palm, a light caress of his compacted balls and she fisted his erection, stroked up and down, then paused, thumbing his penis head's magical softness, encountering moisture she gently spread.

He was perfect.

She bent to take him in her mouth, but he chuckled faintly and she found herself again on her back, wrists pinned over her head.

"I won't last, Mel—"

"Shh." She brought his head down to kiss her. She didn't want him to talk. Every time he did she got that funny feeling, and since everything else about this night had far exceeded her expectations, hell, it had exceeded even her fantasies, she couldn't bear for anything to be less than ideal.

Luckily, she had a surefire way to stop him wanting to talk. She retrieved the condom from under his pillow and managed to close his hand around it. She wasn't sure even with all her experience that she could manage in the dark, and she didn't want to spoil anything by fumbling.

She lay back, listening to the tearing foil, smiling, relaxed, ready. This was all deliciously familiar now. She loved sex. Even when she couldn't come, she loved the sensations, the joining, the broad expanse of a man's back above her, the working of his butt muscles as he pushed inside her. She loved doggy style, missionary, her on top, or both of them in—

He would want to see her again, wouldn't he?

Melanie blew out a silent breath of frustration. *Not now.* Plenty of time later for doubts and worries and—

He was back, hands exploring her more firmly this time, more insistently. His mouth on her breasts involved teeth as well as tongue. He was rougher in his touch, though patient, seeming to read her reactions and needs as if they were a map in front of him.

Incredibly, she responded, desire building again, breath stuttering, hands wandering over his broad masculine shape.

His thighs nudged hers farther apart; she felt the hard head of his erection at her opening and inhaled sharply. Did she say the moment before the first kiss was her favorite? She was changing her mind. This was her favorite, when the real fun was about to begin.

He breathed her name once more, with reverence that cut through her carnal anticipation and made her again uneasy. Only briefly, because he pushed inside her, dug his arms under and around her, and began to make love to her in a way that showed her the phrase wasn't just a euphemism but a literal description, an experience she hadn't known was possible.

Making love.

Afterward—yes, she could come twice within an hour—she

lay in his arms, listening to their breathing return to normal, savoring the contact between them, the delicious skin-on-skin, muscle-pressed-to-muscle afterglow, his hands caressing her hair, her cheek, her shoulder.

"Melanie."

"Not now." She put a finger in the general vicinity of his lips, repositioned it when she hit his chin instead. She was so enveloped in the glow of this moment, so vulnerable to this man and what they'd just shared, that she couldn't handle hearing anything discussed. Not that the sex was good, not that it was bad, not that she should leave now, not what he'd had for dinner, nothing. Because every second spent in conversation would bring them closer to the world of reality, and each word would bring them one word closer to when he let her know it was over. "Later. We'll talk later. Please."

"Okay," he whispered, squeezing her tight, nuzzling a kiss into the sensitive side of her neck.

She sighed, peace spreading through her body, instead of that familiar urge to move on to the next thing, the next activity, the next anything. She was content just to be, in this bed with this man on this perfect, perfect night.

Which, like every other night of her crazy life's adventure, was doomed shortly to end.

2

TRICIA HAWTHORNE SAT in the kitchen she grew up in. Even remodeled, it retained the flavor of her parents, Edith and Edwin Hawthorne. She could remember her mother baking cookies, her father hovering around, eagerly waiting for them to cool. She could remember family dinners around the old table. And she could remember tiptoeing out at midnight on her way to getting drunk. Tiptoeing home drunk at four in the morning, praying neither of her parents would hear her. Sneaking here, sneaking there, doing this, doing that, nothing they ever approved of, behavior that had bewildered and hurt them. Yet they'd loved her, supported her, picked up after her, believing she'd grow out of her wild behavior and settle down.

That only took her until the age of fifty. Good thing her parents were both alive to know their long wait was at an end.

The coffeemaker sputtered out its final drops. Four in the morning… She'd slept only a few hours, finally giving in and resignedly getting up. Tricia had never been a good sleeper, but too many nights were like this now. She'd tried herbal remedies, hypnosis, hot baths, meditation, tapes, relaxation exercises, and finally decided that insomnia was her punishment for a life poorly lived, and that it was just going to be that way until she settled her emotional debts and found inner peace.

She poured her coffee and added skim milk, wishing her waistline and cholesterol count would allow her the luxury of cream. Or one of the enormous bakery blueberry muffins in a plastic container on the counter. She and Melanie were supposed to have breakfast this morning before Melanie went to work, but she hadn't come home last night. Now it was Tricia's turn to worry about her daughter, as her parents and Melanie's older sister, Alana, had been doing for far too long.

Coffee ready, muffins successfully avoided, she sat down on a stool and leaned her elbows on the fancy cream tile counter.

Breakfast with Melanie this morning seemed unlikely to happen now, but Tricia could visit Alana later on, maybe help her unpack boxes. Alana had moved out of this house and in with her boyfriend, Sawyer, the day after they committed to each other—which was also, not coincidentally, Tricia suspected, the day after Tricia had shown up unannounced in Milwaukee. Not that she blamed Alana for holding a grudge. The burden of Tricia's squandered responsibility had fallen on Alana's shoulders until age ten, when Edith and Edwin had taken the girls in, giving up on Tricia's ability to mother them.

Pretty much from the second Alana was born, Tricia had been overwhelmed by what she now understood was practically nonexistent self-esteem due to years of rejecting everything sensible her parents stood for, and instead embracing users and idiots. She'd also been wallowing in the gradual dissolution of her unhealthy relationship with the girls' father, Tom, who had left for good when she was pregnant with Melanie. Reeling from the pain, Tricia had continued to drown herself in alcohol, drugs and other men, telling herself the girls were okay, or, even worse, not considering them at all.

She had wanted her next fix, her next sexual high, always the next thing. Any good that had developed in either daughter was thanks to their grandparents. All Tricia had contributed was damage.

Last year, after she'd been living in California more or less permanently with her men and her art, the death of a close friend's daughter due to a drug overdose on the day Tricia turned fifty had shot home the obvious truth that she wasn't going to have forever to get to know her own kids.

Depression followed, then therapy, various withdrawals, more depression, in the process driving away the latest man she'd shacked up with. Tricia had moved in with a friend — Dahlia, who deserved sainthood for putting up with her—and slowly and surely she'd pulled herself out of the muck of clueless oblivion, limb by limb washed herself with honesty, put on clean dry clothes of self-acceptance, sold everything she couldn't fit in a suitcase except her art supplies, and bought a one-way ticket to Milwaukee.

Now she'd vowed, however long it took, to make amends, to be worthy of forgiveness. She was sober, drug-free, dateless, and determined for the first time in her adult life to *be* an adult. To live a life she and her daughters and her parents could be proud of. A huge and often terrifying goal.

One step at a time. One day at a time.

A key jiggled the back-door lock. The familiar sound catapulted Tricia back to memories of guilty predawn homecomings. The handle turning with a slight rattle. The door opening… Careful! The hinges squeaked if pushed too fast.

Soft footsteps, a hand carrying shoes, door closing, shh, don't let Mom and Dad hear….

Except in this case, there was only Mom, no Dad; the mom was Tricia, while the child sneaking in was her twenty-six-year-old daughter. "Hi, Melanie."

Melanie gasped; her hand flew to her chest, luckily not the one holding her strappy black high-heeled sandals or they would have flown up and smacked her in the head. "Mom. Oh, my gosh, you scared me. What are you doing up at this hour?"

"I could ask you the same thing."

"Oh." She arranged her features into Cautious Liar Mode. Tricia nearly chuckled. Nothing Melanie could pull would be new to her. "I was out late with a girlfriend and—"

"How about the truth?" Tricia sipped her coffee, apparently unconcerned, inside probably ten times more nervous than Melanie. She was never comfortable with authority, and it had been years since she'd had to be a parent. "Saves time for both of us."

Melanie blinked. Frowned. Thumped her shoes onto the floor and sidled up to the counter. "Any more coffee?'

Tricia jerked her head back toward the machine. "Help yourself."

She did, this amazing beautiful woman Tricia knew so little about. Melanie had been a remarkably peaceful baby, a relief after Alana, who had screamed at anything and everything. Tricia had been living with their father for three years before he'd announced he was too young for a family. Instead of marrying her, he was going off to find himself in India.

Lose himself, more likely. She'd never heard from him again.

"Well." Melanie perched on the stool opposite her mother at the counter. Her lips were swollen, chin pink from stubble burn, hair messed, eyes glowing. She could say whatever she wanted, but Tricia knew where she'd been. "Actually, I was with a guy."

"No kidding."

"What?" She touched her face. "How can you tell?"

"A mother always knows." She got through the words with the appropriate deadpan expression, then couldn't help it, let out a snort of laughter.

Melanie's eyes grew rounder, if that were possible. "You do that just like Alana."

"What?"

"That funny laugh."

"Yeah?" She wouldn't let on how it touched her, tortured her, too. How many of their shared family traits had she missed out on discovering? At least it wasn't too late for that. "Is this a guy you've...been with before?"

"First time. He's...amazing." She sighed; her eyes softened. She might as well have had hearts popping out the top of her head.

Tricia's chest ached. *Oh, Melanie.* The pain she'd continue to go through if she didn't stop making men the keepers of her happiness... The latest entry on the long list of ways Tricia had let her daughters down, a list that would inevitably lengthen as she caught up on the years she hadn't been around.

But she was ready. Primed. Strong. Focused. She'd do whatever it took. "If he was that amazing, why did you leave? You could have rescheduled breakfast with me. You know I would have understood."

"Oh." Melanie blushed, looked down at her bright pink mug, decorated with angels and hearts. A Valentine's Day present? From whom? Tricia had missed so much. "I didn't want to skip breakfast with you."

Not entirely true. "And...?"

Her daughter's head jerked up. "And?"

"Melanie. You can't shock me. You have no reason to hide anything from me. There's some other reason you're not telling the truth."

Melanie met her eyes, hers blue like her father's, only gentler. It had been a lot of years since Tricia had looked into them with a clear head. "Mom, are you psychic? Seriously?"

Tricia shrugged. She was, sort of, but enough people had made fun of her that she didn't bother claiming the title anymore. "Call it women's intuition. Now tell me. Why did you leave an amazing guy in the middle of a wonderful night?"

Melanie twisted her mouth, the same way she had when she was small and something confused her. Amazing how little had changed—and how much. "I went to sleep next to him completely blissed out, then I woke up and realized I had to meet you for breakfast, but also…that in the morning, it would be, uh…"

"Morning." Tricia spoke without sarcasm. She understood. "Everything that was safe and mysterious and beautiful in the dark, blurred by alcohol, would be stark and over-lit and real. And hard. And I'm not talking about the guy's you-know-what."

Melanie interrupted her shocked look with a giggle. "Yes. Yes, that's it. How did you know?"

Tricia answered by lifting her eyebrow. *Think, Melanie.*

Her face fell. "Oh, right. You're the expert."

"Was. I'm not proud of it."

Melanie lifted her chin, again a stubborn three-year-old. "*I'm* not ashamed of what I do."

"I'm not asking you to be. I wish I'd lived my life differently. That has nothing to do with you or how you live yours."

"True." She took another sip of coffee.

"What's his name?"

"Stoner." Said defensively. "He's the brother of…a good friend and coworker. Edgar. Edgar Raymond."

"Stoner, huh?" Tricia watched her daughter curiously. No problem talking about Stoner. But Edgar… "You seeing him again?"

Melanie shrugged, eyes on the counter. "He was asleep when I left."

"I'm sure he knows how to find you." Tricia finished her coffee in silence. She had a lot more to say about all this, but she wasn't good at motherhood yet, maybe she never would be, and she wanted to think things over before stumbling into any blunders when her reconciliation with her daughters was still so raw and new. "I'm going to shower. Then we can go out later on."

"How about Ted's on Sixty-second Street? It's a great greasy spoon."

"Hey, I'm a native, too." Tricia smiled, slighted even though she didn't blame her daughter for forgetting. "I know Ted's."

"Right." Melanie nodded, looking embarrassed and so beautiful Tricia wanted to hug her and kiss her smooth cheek, so different from the plump baby one she'd kissed so often—there were some redeeming memories. But she didn't know how Melanie would react, and she wasn't going to risk affection this early into their reunion.

"See you soon." She put her cup in the sink, went down the narrow hallway and climbed the stairs, thinking that after her shower she'd take a few minutes to meditate over the problem with Melanie, see if the collective unconscious had any advice to offer.

Alana's path through life didn't worry her too much. But Melanie's…Melanie needed maternal intervention.

And though it was ironic, given that Tricia was exactly the type of mother who'd caused Melanie to have this problem in the first place, she was also exactly the type of mother who could help her daughter change her life for the better.

EDGAR WOKE UP KNOWING something was wrong. No, not wrong, something had happened. Something huge, something—

Melanie.

He opened his eyes. The space next to him in bed was empty. No Melanie.

Damn it. He'd dreamed about spending a night with her

many times—plenty while he was awake. This time he'd swear their being together had really happened.

Hadn't it?

He rubbed his forehead, trying to clear his fuzzy brain. On the one hand nothing could be less likely. He'd known Melanie two years and been in love with her for both of them. In all that time she'd never given him more than a sisterly glance. So for her to jump into his bed out of the blue and seduce him made about as much sense as conservatives voting for huge tax hikes.

Except...last week sitting with Melanie on the couch in this apartment, right before Stoner had walked in and made Melanie's jaw go slack, just before that, she'd been saying something about wanting to date a different type of guy, giving Edgar real hope for the first time.

Maybe he wasn't crazy?

He had to be crazy.

He blinked, struggled up, then on impulse leaned down to inhale over the pillow she'd used to see if traces of her scent lingered.

Yes. Oh, my God, yes. He was instantly hard again. She'd really been here. His most potent sexual fantasy and his deepest emotional fantasy—both came true in one mind-blowing unexpected night.

But how? Why?

Maybe she was still here? Eating breakfast? Using the bathroom? Watching TV? He got out of bed, stepped into a pair of gray boxers and walked through the apartment. Stoner hadn't come home. What a gratifying non-surprise. Last night Edgar had dutifully been getting ready to bunk down in the sofa bed when he'd realized that if Stoner followed his usual pattern after a night out with his band, he wouldn't be back until morning. Damned if Edgar would spend another lumpy, restless night while his comfortable queen-size bed lay empty.

He finished his rounds. No Melanie, not that he really

expected she'd still be here. But also no note. No messages. No "Thanks for last night, it was the best time of my entire life. Call me ASAP. I love you. Melanie."

Right.

His heart sank. The queen of the one-nighters had bolted.

Except she had to know by now how he felt about her. He'd dropped plenty of hints, even made up a girlfriend, Emma, so Melanie would feel more at ease with him. Amazing how close a skittish woman would let a guy get when there was no threat of a relationship developing. And amazing what that guy could get away with saying to said skittish woman when he was supposedly safely attached. Edgar had said it all.

She had to know. Especially once she found out Emma wasn't real. She'd have put it together. And there was no way Melanie would mess with his head so extremely by showing up in his bed, then ditching him. She was neither that cold nor that desperate.

The real Emma, his black cat, jumped gracefully down from the bookcase and fixed him with a feed-me-or-die stare.

He fed her, glancing at the clock. Early still. He could work out now in case Melanie wanted to go out after work.

Adrenaline burned through his system, bliss and torture in equal measures. He'd been patient so far. Knowing Melanie, he'd have to be even more patient now, when he was the most eager for a continuation of what they'd started last night.

If they *had* started anything last night.

Had they?

He wasn't the kind of guy she usually went for, which was the understatement of the millennium. That fact could work in his favor now. Because he didn't fit any of her hot-guy criteria, maybe she'd been after more than a quick lay. Maybe she was even open to that most terrifying of all things as far as Melanie was concerned—A Relationship.

Down, boy. He couldn't get ahead of himself like this; he'd only drive himself crazy with tantalizing hope, and in the process set himself up for a huge and potentially castrating fall. He needed to prepare to hear from Melanie that last night was a nutty aberration, both a beginning and an end.

Or she could come through the office door with a special secret smile meant only for him.

God, he was going to have to jerk off if he thought about that any more.

He went into the spare room where he kept his treadmill and weights, and spent an hour trying to calm himself down with exhaustion. It didn't work. He could have spent the rest of the day lifting and running and still have enough nervous energy left over to power a rocketship.

Out of the shower, he made himself eggs, whole-grain toast and a banana yogurt shake, sat at the breakfast nook and could barely eat.

Damn. He was a wreck. A geeky pathetic wreck in love with a woman who went through men like doctors went through latex gloves.

But he was also a geeky pathetic wreck in love with a woman who'd slipped into his bed and allowed him to show her every bit of that love, who'd responded, trembled in his arms, climaxed twice, and gone to sleep calmer and more relaxed than he'd ever known her to be, as if she understood as clearly as he did that she'd come home.

If only she'd stayed...

The apartment door burst open, making him jump, but for once he was glad Stoner forgot to lock up when he left, or Melanie wouldn't have been able to get in last night and surprise him, practically to the point of cardiac arrest.

"Hey." His brother looked like hell, cheeks stubbled, skin pale, eyes ringed dark.

"G'morning. Good time last night?"

"The best, man." He high-fived Edgar on his way to the refrigerator. "I'm parched this morning, though. Parched."

"There's more juice in the cupboard if you want it."

"Thanks. How was your evening?"

"The usual." If he'd been with anyone but Melanie, he would have given in to his pride and told his brother what really happened, maybe gotten up for a manly, growling chest bump or two.

But no one would know what went on with Melanie until he was damn sure all of it would happen again. Repeatedly.

"You gotta come hear me play, dude." Stoner finished the carton of OJ and belched impressively.

"I'll come to a rehearsal. I'm not into the club scene. Crowds, smoke, noise… It's not my thing."

"Geez, Eddie, you gotta *live*."

Edgar didn't bother mentioning that living the way Stoner did would make him feel half-dead most of the time. "I live. Just not your way."

"More like *Pater* and *Mater*."

"If you mean cleaning happens, yeah. If you mean I'd rather hear a symphony or jazz band than garage band rock, again yeah. If you mean I live only to impress other people with my possessions and my good taste, then no."

"Boom, you got 'em. Don't know how they stand the charade."

Edgar shrugged. "They're surrounded by it in that town. Hard to escape."

"No kidding. It's like a science dish. Petri. Swarming with obscenely rich bacteria."

Edgar chuckled. "Stoner, that was sheer poetry."

"Yeah?" He narrowed his eyes thoughtfully. "There's a song in there. Gotta think about that one later."

"You been in touch with Mom and Dad lately?" Edgar asked casually, but he knew they both worried when they didn't hear.

"I mean to. I just forget." He tossed the juice carton into the trash. "Hey, I saw your friend Melanie last night at The Wicked Hop."

"Yeah?" Edgar managed not to look smug. "She goes there a lot after work."

"She told me. Hot chick. Great ass."

"Huh." He ate toast to avoid talking about her, uh, finer points with Stoner.

"I was going to see if she and I could hook up later, but then I got all into the party where I was." He shoved a couple of pieces of bread in the toaster. "Tell her I said hey, and sorry last night didn't work out."

"Sure." Edgar stacked his plates, hiding a smirk. As far as he was concerned, last night had definitely worked out. "I'll tell her."

"So what's the plan today, bro?"

Edgar set his plates and cup in the dishwasher. "I work, remember? Every day? Big office? Cubicles? Paychecks?"

"Right, right. Have fun with that."

"I'm sure I will."

He brushed his teeth, gathered a few disks and files he'd need at the office, and glanced at the clock. Early, but he couldn't wait to get to work and see how Melanie would react to him, whether she'd acknowledge their intense connection of the night before or whether she'd balk. Either way, she couldn't erase what they'd shared, which gave him a better chance than ever of winning her.

Winning Melanie. He wanted to break into a crazed dance at the mere thought.

He pictured her waking up this morning craving more of him the same way he'd woken up craving more of her, wishing she'd conquered her fears in the middle of the night and stayed with him.

It could happen. Miracles did.

And if that was the case, then why not order up another, so he could be with her again tonight?

3

EDGAR PUSHED OPEN THE door to Caffe Coffee, his every-morning java shop on Chicago Street; halfway between his apartment and work. Melanie couldn't live without Starbucks' mocha frappuccino but he preferred the organic Blue Mountain here, flown from a family farm in Jamaica, roasted on the premises, brewed by his favorite barista, Kaitlin, just the way he liked it—strong enough to dissolve paint. He could make the same coffee at home, but the croissants at Caffe Coffee were nearly as good as the ones he'd loved so much in Paris, and the ritual of coming here every morning appealed to him. So did Kaitlin. She was the kind of little sister he would have liked to have, serious and shy, with a dry sense of humor that hit when you least expected it.

Lately, though, he'd been starting to wonder, by the way her light brown eyes lit when he walked in, by the way she lingered to chat even when customers were behind him in line, that she might have ideas concerning him that weren't exactly sisterly.

Oh, the irony. Kaitlin was sweet, funny and in his league, a student at Marquette University, studying marketing. But even on a normal day, he was so full of Melanie he couldn't imagine dating Kaitlin. Today…well, he'd considered skipping today's visit, but he knew Melanie would be late to work, and he'd sit in his cubicle for what seemed like forever, a nervous wreck waiting for her. Better to stop for coffee and delay that agony by a few minutes.

Not that caffeine would do much to calm his nerves.

"Hi, Edgar!" Kaitlin had his coffee ready—he didn't have the heart to say he wanted half-decaf this morning. "Croissant today?"

"Not today, Kaitlin, thanks."

"I was thinking about you last night." She snapped the lid on his cup and rang up the purchase.

"Really?" He wasn't thinking about her last night.

"I saw that movie you recommended. *Cane Toads?*" She giggled. "You're right. It was hysterical."

"Glad you enjoyed it." He handed over a five, wishing he could have fallen for someone uncomplicated like Kaitlin instead of beating his head against Melanie's brick wall for so long. He hoped he'd survive until she showed up at work. His heart was already beating so hard he was afraid it would give out, classic heart attack in the middle of the shop. He should probably pour his coffee down the office sink. "Pretty odd cast of characters, wasn't it?"

"Yes! Where did they find those people?" She put the change into his hand, her fingers lingering.

He was getting even more anxious. From her touch, from his guilt that he might be encouraging her by showing up every day, from the sudden fear that Melanie might have come in early today and he was missing her. What if she was so eager to see him again after last night that—

"I, um, was wondering…" Kaitlin glanced at whoever was behind him, and leaned forward so her words wouldn't carry.

Instinctive panic. She was going to ask him out. He couldn't handle this. Not today.

"Listen, thanks for the coffee, Kaitlin. As always." He

spoke loudly, pretending he hadn't heard the beginning of her sentence. "I'll see you tomorrow."

"Oh, um…" Her eyes dropped. "Yeah, I…okay."

Smiling, he backed away a few steps, waved and turned, feeling like a schmuck. A prime schmuck. Why couldn't she have asked him another day, when he wasn't completely insane to be near Melanie?

Because there weren't any days like that. He knew he was obsessed; he knew his feelings weren't rational or smart or probably even sane. No woman had ever affected him like this—okay, not since junior high school, when crazed hormones made obsession the norm. No woman *should* affect him like this. He understood about balance, about healthy infatuation gone too far; he knew all of it. But try convincing his id.

He left, feeling Kaitlin staring wistfully at his back, imagining the customer behind him already annoyed that his barista was not baristing.

Why Melanie? He'd asked himself over and over again. He didn't know. He only knew he had a solid-as-rock conviction that she was the woman for him, and nothing, no amount of talking to himself or reading self-help books, had been able to shake it.

After last night…well, this morning, Melanie could, with a single glance, wipe out every long-dormant hope that had sprung ecstatically to life the previous night.

Forget heart attack. He'd have a stroke and be a vegetable the rest of his life.

Luckily, the morning was cool and refreshing, so he could arrive at work a nervous wreck, yes, but not a sweaty nervous wreck.

He pushed through the front door of Triangle Graphics, greeting Anna, the receptionist, who was stationed in front of a huge analog clock.

Eight forty-five.

If Melanie showed up at her usual time, nine-thirty at the very earliest, that gave him forty-five minutes to find out if he'd be the happiest man on the planet or the most broken.

He strode down the short hall to the open room where the graphic designers worked, including Melanie; said good morning to Todd Maniscotto, his and Melanie's boss; nodded to Jenny, Melanie's good friend; sat at his cubicle, which was right next to Melanie's.

Melanie. Melanie. Melanie.

Roughly forty-minutes later, thinking he could expect Melanie any second, he checked his watch to find it was actually roughly five minutes later.

Not heart attack, not stroke; aneurism. One big pop in his brain and done, before he knew what was happening.

He opened the file he'd been working on last night before he went home, ate dinner alone, went to bed and was awakened by the sexiest woman alive sliding into his bed and...

Get a grip, Edgar.

Where was he? Working on a sporting goods catalog for Premium Sports. Today's challenge: how to make a package of golf tees look like the sexiest product in the world.

Paint Melanie's picture on it?

Grip, Edgar, remember?

He grappled with the tees and won, rotated a baseball mitt this way and that, changed the text to wrap more snugly around it, all with a few clicks of his mouse.

As convenient and time-saving as computers were, part of Edgar couldn't help romanticizing the idea of Man at His Drafting Table, like his architect father, pencils sharp, straightedges handy. He'd grown up playing trucks around his dad's legs, since his father had worked around the clock. Whenever Dad had taken time off, he'd sit blinking at his family in surprise as if he couldn't quite figure out how they had gotten there.

"Good morning, Ralph." He heard Melanie's voice down at the end of the line of cubicles.

Edgar fumbled with his mouse, selected something he shouldn't have, reached to fix it and hit the wrong button on his keyboard; his computer started shutting down.

Damn it. Edgar, the epitome of cool. No wonder Melanie had been able to resist him for so long.

A glance at his watch while he tried to steady his breathing. Nine-fifteen. Early for her. Good sign? Bad sign?

Hang on, Edgar, you'll know all too soon.

Her perfume rounded the corner of his cubicle a split second before she did. Just the scent had him buzzing with arousal. She'd been everything he dreamed of in bed. No, everything and more because his dreams had been dreams and last night she'd been real.

"Morning, Eddie."

"Hey." He grinned up at her, as tenderly as he dared, knowing no matter how she felt underneath, she'd still be skittish this morning. Whatever had made her bolt in the middle of the night wouldn't have resolved itself this soon. And with their coworkers all around, she couldn't exactly launch into praises of his sexual technique or drop to her knees and confess undying love. Which was a damn shame.

But she'd have to give some sign, wouldn't she?

God, she was beautiful. Yawning, clutching her Starbucks cup, hair disheveled as if someone had been tangling his fingers through it all night in order to kiss her as often as possible. Her lips were dark, chin pink from his stubble. He hated to think he'd hurt her at all, but the man part of him—yes, there was a man part even to him—enjoyed a cheap macho thrill that he'd left his mark.

She wore a clingy rose-colored knee-length skirt that molded itself to her gorgeous thighs. Her ass looked firm and strong underneath and he nearly sighed when she sat, and he lost the view. Last night his hands had been a-a-ll over that—

He had to stop thinking about it right now.

Or else he was going to stand up, yank the skirt up those strong soft thighs, lift her onto the desk, step between her legs and—

He had to stop thinking about that right now.

Or else he was going to—

"How was Chicago?"

He blinked. Back to earth. How was what? "Chicago?"

"Hello? Edgar?" She leaned down, smiling, waved in front of his face. "Last night? Remember?"

He remembered every second. "Oh, yes."

"So…?"

He was lost. "So what?"

"Tell me how it was."

He stared blankly. "I don't…"

"You know, *Chicago?*"

Chicago? Was that her code word for what they'd done? So they could talk about it in the office and no one would guess? Very odd. She was not acting the way he expected. "It was… God, Melanie, it was fabulous. The best night of my life."

"Wow. That's…wow. Great." She tipped her head, looking a little surprised. "What made it so great?"

"Uh…" He was not really sure he liked this game. "The sights. The, um, sensations. And really, most of all the… emotions. More than I've ever felt in…Chicago."

"Oh. Well. I'm glad you had fun." Her eyes narrowed. He'd said something wrong. She'd blindsided him with all this coded talk; he was hopelessly confused. And hopelessly in love with her.

What else was new?

"Edgar." She leaned closer to whisper, her shy smile so sweet he could barely keep from kissing her. Last night those lips had belonged to him. He still couldn't get over it. He probably never would. "I had a fabulous night, too."

His heart rose like a rocket, the hope almost as painful as the countless rejections. "Yeah?"

"Mmm, yeah."

Oh, dear God. He was getting hard again, not the best place or time. But this was everything he'd hoped for. Melanie, acknowledging what went on between them, admitting she enjoyed it. "You had a good time, huh?"

"Ohh, yes." She blushed. "You know what I mean, right?"

"I do."

Her smile turned a little anxious. "I hope it's okay with you."

"It's more than okay, Melanie." He was whispering, too; his passion for her made voice impossible. "It's what I've dreamed of for the last two years."

Her shy smile froze. She looked as if she'd eaten something rotten. "Uh…really?"

Crap. *Crap.* He'd gone too far. He had to remember whom he was talking to. That she wasn't in the same emotional place he was. That letting herself be so open to him was undoubtedly a new and frightening experience. If he pushed too hard now, this soon after the breakthrough, she could bolt.

"Okay, not *everything* I've dreamed of." His laugh came out goofy and strained.

She didn't seem to mind. In fact, her face relaxed and she laughed, too, considerably more musically than he had.

"Well, I'm glad you approve. I wouldn't want anything to upset our friendship, Edgar."

His heart sank. Lower than he thought possible. *Friendship?*

No way. No effing way. What went on between them last night was *not* friendship no matter what she wanted to tell herself this morning. It was not friends with benefits, it was not getting their rocks off just for the hell of it. What they had last night was everything sex with love should be. And if she blew it off like it was another romp in the hay, he was going to check himself into a psychiatric hospital. Or have *her* committed.

"I think we're talking a hell of a lot more than friendship, Melanie." His voice actually came out with strength.

"Whah?" She looked bewildered.

"Last night. It was not about friendship."

"Oh, no." Her face cleared. "No, Stoner and I aren't friends, not the way you and I are. Nor will we ever be, I'm sure. Don't worry."

He gaped at her. "Why would I worry whether you're friends with Stoner?"

She gaped back. "I mean, after I was with him last night."

Last night? With Stoner?

No, no, wait, Stoner had mentioned he'd bumped into her. "You mean when you saw him in the bar?"

"Ed-gar." She rolled her eyes. "What is with you this morning? *No*, not in the bar, afterward, in your bedroom."

"What does that have to do with Sto—" The rest of his brother's name refused to leave his lips. This morning Stoner had said a planned late-night date with Melanie hadn't worked out. Melanie had been worrying that sex with his brother would affect her friendship with Edgar. Her ugly, dorky buddy, Edgar.

"Excuse me." He got up, staggered across the room, nearly knocking down his boss, coming out of his office.

Todd looked concerned. "Edgar? Something wrong?"

Yes! Everything! "No. Nothing. I'm fine." Suicidal, maybe, but nothing serious.

Luckily, there was no one in the men's room. He made a beeline for a stall, horribly afraid he was going to be sick.

Melanie had thought she was screwing Stoner last night.

She didn't know she'd been making love to him. All that passion, all that emotion, all that sweetness between them...

A dream after all.

He wanted to puke even if his body wasn't ready to. Melanie *hadn't* come to him; there was no miracle there. Of course not. She'd come to his brother, the sex god, the hot masculine jerk without a shred of depth, without much intelligence, without room in his monstrous head to care about anyone but himself.

Melanie's type all over. What had Edgar been thinking? How could he even have imagined she'd crawl into bed with *him?*

Stoner had bumped into her at the bar, invited her up to Edgar's room, Edgar's bed, knowing Edgar would be sleeping on the couch so as not to inconvenience his brother.

Chicago? That would be Stoner's invention. Which helped only a little, knowing at least Melanie hadn't come into his apartment expecting to step over Edgar on the sofa bed and then screw his brother's brains out a few feet away.

He leaned back against the partition, making himself breathe slowly and carefully until the urge to lose his breakfast subsided. This was worse than when he'd introduced Melanie to his jewelry-artist downstairs neighbor, Sledge, in order to buy her one of his pieces. Sledge repaid him by hitting on Melanie and then telling Edgar all about it. This was much worse. His own damn brother, who had everything Edgar didn't—except brains and integrity, which didn't count for enough in this world.

Edgar had grown up invisible to women, one of those kids fawned over by adults, a "good worker," a "great help to his parents," a "responsible citizen," while his mess of a brother was like a bug zapper for the female sex. One after another, drawn to his light and his high voltage, zap, zap, zap, they went up in blue smoke one after another, the destruction of so many not slowing the lineup at all. While "responsible citizen" Edgar sat on the sidelines in awed misery.

This time it was his heart that got busted, not his ego.

Zap.

He turned to the wall, took a few more deep breaths; the cold metal felt good against his forehead. Solid. Impartial. Calming.

Okay, Edgar. Deal with facts. Fact: Melanie hadn't known in the dark that he was himself. Fact: they'd had incredible sex. Fact: she'd left in the middle of the night, which he happened to know she didn't usually do, because generally she was hopeful the relationship would continue and she wanted to be around in daylight. So something had been different last night for her.

That was good. He'd concentrate on that. Regardless of whom she'd thought he was, she'd experienced emotion so intense she'd ducked out rather than face it. Which meant that on some level, however subconscious, she had feelings for him. Only she didn't know it yet.

Therefore, logically, all Edgar had to do was go out there and tell her she'd been with him last night. Make sure she knew he was an innocent party in this, explain the bed mix-up. She'd be shocked at first, but then her wheels would start turning, she'd remember what it had been like with him, Edgar, and she'd come around. She'd realize—she had to realize—that they were meant to be together. And once she realized that…

There would be nothing stopping them.

He lifted his head and grinned at his homely face, mind whirling, stomach at peace. He'd get to be with her again, maybe tonight. Those eyes, those lips, that body…

Edgar closed his eyes and groaned, tortured by his so-long-yearned-for happiness now so closely within reach.

Only one more thing to do.

He straightened, splashed water on his face, washed his hands. Tried to tamp down his mess of wiry hair.

Okay.

Out of the men's room, he walked back to his cubicle, one step at a time, adrenaline buzzing so loudly through his system he felt as if he were operating in a different dimension from the rest of the office.

When he rounded the corner, Melanie looked up in concern, saved her file and turned her chair to face him. "Are you okay? I'm really sorry if this has upset you. You could have told me right out that you didn't want me with your brother, you didn't have to pretend—"

"Melanie." He sat, scootched his chair close to hers, took her hand. He was just going to say it. "Last night. In bed. That wasn't Stoner. That was me."

She raised her eyebrows expectantly, waiting for the punch line. He didn't crack a smile.

The eyebrows sank slowly. "Edgar...don't do that. It's not funny."

"I'm serious. It was me. It was dark, so you didn't realize, and I thought..."

She took her hand away, eyes widening. Understanding dawned on her face, then rose and rose into full-blown horror. Not shock, not surprise, but horror. As if he'd just told her she'd slept with a person with active cases of every known STD. Or with her brother. Or with her dog.

He waited. Waited for the horror to change to surprise, for those wheels to start turning, for her to connect the man in front of her with the passion and tenderness, the wild erotic chemistry, the panting straining desperate need to join and climax, and for that surprise to soften her expression, to part her lips, *Oh, Edgar, that was you!*

None of that happened. She continued to stare as if she couldn't imagine anything more disgusting than lying naked with him.

Okay. He'd wait longer. She had to make the connection soon. Tick…tick…tick…

Still nothing.

He couldn't bear it. Not one more ticking, torturous second of this pain or this humiliation, not one.

A forced laugh, as real as he could make it. "Gotcha."

Her laughter wasn't forced. It was loud and long and full of so much relief that his pain, which he'd been pretty sure was as bad as it could get, got worse.

"Oh, my God, Edgar. You really had me. Ha!" She put her hand to her chest. "Damn. That would have been really, really—"

He must have shown something in his face to stop her. Something. Because thank God she did stop, and looked confused and contrite.

"Horrible?"

"No, oh, no, Edgar. No. Of course not. It's just that you and I…" She laughed again. Uncomfortable this time. He was glad. He wanted her to suffer, even just a little. "We're not about…that."

"Right." She was wrong. She was so damn wrong, he wanted to jump up and bellow it, beat his chest and fling furniture around the office.

But that wasn't him. He was sweet, gentle Edgar, who let the world walk all over him rather than trip people up to get what he wanted. Who adored this woman unreasonably and would do anything rather than make her unhappy.

So she'd go on being wrong, and he'd go on being her best friend, and she'd probably go on and try to screw Stoner again. And even when she did and the sex was bad compared to what they'd shared, even when she put two and two together as she writhed in bed with his brother and realized Edgar really *had* been in bed with her last night…

At least he wouldn't be there to see that look of sick horror on her face ever, ever again.

4

"THIS WAS MADE FOR YOU." Melanie held a pretty teal cotton sweater up to her sister. The color would look gorgeous with Alana's dark hair.

Nose wrinkled, Alana gave the top a once-over. Melanie wanted to growl at her. She wasn't wild about shopping with her sister under any circumstances, but since the trip had been Mom's idea, Alana was being even less cooperative than usual. If she'd found the same top herself she'd love it.

"Yes! That is really cute. Alana, try it on, I want to see." Tricia smiled so hard it looked painful. Melanie wished she'd relax and let Alana come to her when she was ready.

"Thanks, it's not really me." Alana walked to another section. Melanie turned away, embarrassed for her sister, hurting for her mother. Maybe Alana would never be ready, which was stupid.

They were at Wauwatosa's Mayfair Mall, attempting to have a fun girls' shopping day over way too complicated undercurrents. They probably should have stayed home.

But since they hadn't, Melanie browsed the racks determinedly, trying to find something else Alana would like, and something Mom would like, and while she was at it, how about something Stoner would like on Melanie?

No matter how hard she tried to stop it, her brain played a constant soundtrack: *Stoner, Stoner, Stoner, Stoner.*

She burned for him, in a way she hadn't ever burned for a guy except when he was right in front of her, taking off his clothes. It wasn't just the sex, either, though mmm, no complaints there. It was that feeling. That emotion, that sense that they belonged to each other, that she was his most cherished possession, and he hers.

Melanie was falling in love. For real.

Yeah, she'd thought she was falling in love for real before. A dozen or so men had made the cut, but this time...this time it *was* for real. For one thing, she wasn't telling anyone, and all the other times she couldn't trumpet her passion loudly enough to enough people. And...well, she just knew.

The thought scared her but excited her, too. Wasn't it about time? She was twenty-six, with too many lovers in her past. Maybe all of them had led her to Stoner, all those disappointments made her more able to recognize the real thing when it smacked her.

The terrifying possibility did remain that he wasn't in love with her. How could he not be? Without words, everything he did had said it loud and clear all night long.

I love you, Melanie.

"You have got to be kidding me."

Melanie started and realized she was holding up an orange-and-green-striped blouse with ruffles, staring absently, not seeing a thing while she enjoyed her fantasy. Alana had busted her. "It's beautiful! It will go perfectly with your orange eyes and green hair, sister dear."

"Ha-ha."

"Alana, how about this?" Tricia held up a soft pink sweater with a dipping neckline and diagonal, alternating smooth and pebbled-knit stripes. "You can dress it up for a foundation meeting or dress it down for a date. Sexy, but not provocative."

Silence while Alana contemplated whether nursing her hostility was worth passing up a gorgeous sweater. Melanie goosed her firmly.

"Yeah, it's nice." She took the sweater from their mother and marched to the dressing room.

Melanie gave her mom a thumbs-up and a weak grin. She didn't want to get stuck in the middle of this battle. Tricia had been a terrible mother, but…she was trying to make amends. Second chances were important, so Melanie would swallow her anger and get to know Tricia as a friend at least. She hoped Alana would eventually do likewise.

"Have you been in touch with Stoner yet?"

"Uh…no." She ran her hands over a rack of skirts, loving the feel of soft material under her fingers. "I'm letting him make the next move."

"Which he hasn't done."

"Mom, it's only been two days. I can't crowd him."

"In my experience, when a man wants you, there is no mistaking it."

"He's…busy." Her fear ran deeper. He couldn't disappear, not like the others. Maybe Melanie had been with too many men, but she knew when sex was more than just sex, because she'd had so much that was nothing more. Sometimes it was even less.

"What's up with this Edgar guy?"

"Edgar?" She felt all jumbled up at the question. "Why do you ask that?"

Tricia shrugged and pulled out a pair of soft gray dress pants, frowned, and put them back. "Just curious. You guys have been friends for a while, right?"

"A couple of years." She extracted a flowered sundress from the crowded sale rack, feeling light-headed and strange. Kind of how she'd felt when Edgar had made that completely bizarre joke about him being the one in bed with her two nights ago. She couldn't imagine many things more unsettling than making love to one man, then finding out he'd been someone else. Added to that, there was no way she could connect the goofy, lovable guy that was Edgar with the sexual Adonis she'd been writhing all over the previous night.

And yet…if it *had* been Ed? That's where things got *really* unsettling. She'd felt panicky and disoriented, excited and terrified. The relief when he admitted he was joking had been as overwhelming as the complicated feelings she'd just been fighting through. "He's a good guy."

"Seems like. Ever think of dating him?"

"No. No." The denial was quick and automatic, then Melanie laughed, realizing that wasn't quite true. "Well, sort of. I mean I thought I *should* date him because he's nice, but one look at his brother, boom, there went that idea. You know me."

"Hmm."

"Hmm?" Melanie had started perspiring. Did they turn off the air-conditioning in the store? "What, hmm?"

"It's that when you talk about him, you—"

"What do you think?" Alana strutted over, modeling the sweater, which did all the right things in all the right places for her figure and brought out the color in her cheeks. Love-color.

"You're beautiful." Melanie couldn't help a wistful sigh. Even if Alana had been wearing the green-and-orange shirt she'd be beautiful. Melanie had never seen her happier than since she'd met Sawyer. Okay, maybe not at first. At that initial meeting, he'd just moved in with Melanie because he needed a place to stay, and Alana had barreled up from Chicago to "save" her baby sister from a guy she'd assumed was Melanie's next user jerk boyfriend. And, yeah, maybe Melanie had sort of given her the idea that she and Sawyer were involved… um, actually…engaged. Matrimony had been Melanie's goal, anyway, but she couldn't summon anything for Sawyer other than sisterly affection. So poor Alana had first met him when

Sawyer crawled into her bed in the middle of the night by mistake. At the time Alana had been more furious and out-raged than happy. Not only because of that but because she'd thought he was dating Melanie and couldn't understand why he kept coming on to her. Eventually, of course, she had fallen, and how.

Melanie always fell first and became furious and outraged later. Maybe she needed to try it the other way around.

Except Stoner...Stoner was different. She felt him in her heart, whereas most of her previous passions she felt mostly in her fantasies and, to put it bluntly, between her legs.

"That's a sale. You're lovely, Alana."

"Thanks." Alana managed a tight smile at her mother and strode back to the changing room.

Tricia sighed. "She's a tough one."

"Give her time. Having you back for more than a quick visit is still new for us."

"I know. I just wish..." She trailed off, looking wistfully after Alana.

"Hey, Mom." Melanie glanced at her, then away, uncom-fortable sharing personal stuff with Tricia, but determined to change that. "We're both grown-ups now, but we're also still your girls. We're struggling with how to get those two sides to co-exist."

Tricia gave Melanie a quick hug that left her surprised and pleased. "You are very wise..."

"Ha. I don't—"

"...except when it comes to men."

Melanie sighed. "Ya think?"

"I can help you." She leaned back to examine Melanie's face, hers still mostly unlined and beautiful. "For once I can help you. If you'll let me."

"Thanks, Mom. That's really sweet." Melanie extracted herself gently and turned back to browsing clothes. The last thing she wanted was help from someone who was an even bigger screwup with men than she was. "But this time I've got it right."

Her mother stood next to her, absently fingering dresses. "When you talk about Edgar, something changes in your face and voice."

"Oh, really?" Her voice quavered strangely. They had definitely turned off the store's air-conditioning. "Well, I love Edgar."

"That's what I mean."

"*No,* not like that." Melanie forced a laugh, ha-ha-ha, and took a midcalf yellow-and-blue dress with a halter neck and plunging vee off the rack, hoping Mom would accept a change of subject. Talking about Edgar felt raw after that strange conversation at work yesterday. "How about this for you, Mom? It's tasteful but has a good hit of sexiness. The new you."

She wouldn't mention that most of Tricia's life she'd dressed like either a hooker or a hippie. Her recent overdue acknowledgment of her age had made for a definite wardrobe improvement. Today she wore a simple cream linen shirt with rose-beige cropped pants and looked casually elegant, but still way-hot. A mom any daughter would be proud to be seen with. Another first.

"Ooh, yes, I like." Tricia took the dress, checked the tag and rolled her eyes. "Size six? Bless you, but how about a ten?"

"Ten. Coming up." She found the size and handed it over. "You look like a six."

"Flatterer." She grinned. "Keep it up and I might even ignore the obvious way you dodged talking about Edgar."

"Dodging talking about Edgar? Why?" Alana, back from the changing room, held up a short blue pleated skirt with a matching waist-skimming sleeveless top. "This was made for you, Melanie."

"Ooh, it's adorable!" Melanie immediately pictured herself in the outfit on her next date with Stoner. Which reminded her it had been half an hour since she last checked for messages. She'd forced herself to keep the intervals that long so she wouldn't start feeling too anxious. She'd left him a casual friendly phone message the day before saying she was at The Wicked Hop with Jenny in case he wanted to stop by again. Then she'd spent the entire evening staring at the door. Jenny had finally cashed it in early, not that Melanie could blame her. She'd been terrible company.

No answer from Stoner. Maybe he had a gig last night. Or tonight. She couldn't remember his schedule.

He'd call. He'd be in touch. No worries there. Men didn't process time the same way women did. Women counted every second between text messages, phone calls, dates, imagined every possible aspect of every possible feeling the guy could be having, and drove themselves crazy over it. Men just were. Lucky bastards.

"Try it on." Alana shoved the outfit at her. "And I repeat, why would you dodge talking about Edgar?"

Melanie took the hangers, feeling that odd shakiness again. "Mom has this idea that I'm in love with him."

"Really." Alana's eyes zeroed in on hers with such intensity that she got even more jittery.

"Give me a break. Both of you. Edgar is a friend, period. That's all he'll ever be. Stoner on the other hand..." Her voice thickened. "Is someone really special."

"Uh-huh." Alana rolled her eyes. "I feel I know Stoner just by the lovely sound of his name. Go try that outfit on. I have to go soon. I'm meeting Sawyer in half an hour. I want to see you in it."

"Oh." Tricia sounded disappointed. "I thought we could all have lunch. My treat."

"Sorry." Alana's lips twisted in what was apparently supposed to be a smile. "Not today."

"Sure. Right. Okay." Tricia turned away to a rack of swimsuits.

Melanie sent Alana a silent glare of disapproval. Her sister shrugged, defensive and cranky, probably partly from guilt.

Life was complicated.

"I'm going to try this on." Melanie jerked her head urgently toward their mother, indicating that Alana should go talk to her. Then she practically ran to the dressing room, avoiding the mirror until the skirt and top were completely zipped and snapped, thinking how odd it was that Alana and her tastes had coincided for once. Melanie wasn't becoming more conservative. Maybe Alana was loosening up. They had Sawyer to thank for that.

Three-two-one. Melanie turned. Oh, yes. The skirt and top were made for her. Not slutty but definitely hot. Her legs looked long, her boobs actually counted for something, and the color suited her skin.

Sold. She couldn't stop smiling, turning one way, then the other, imagining Stoner's gentle, strong hands on her, imagining them taking off the top. He had the most incredible touch, lingering and sensual yet masculine and possessive. Taking what he wanted, yet making her feel she was giving it all.

She was getting hot just thinking about it.

Her cell rang. She yanked it out of her bag to peer at the number, and clutched the phone to her chest in a grateful prayer before she answered. *Stoner.*

Okay, Melanie. Keep it casual. Keep it cool. Keep it together. Guys like Stoner didn't want to know you were falling in love with them after one night. She had to act as if she didn't much care if she ever saw him again. Why she had to play that stupid game she'd never understood, but she'd learned the painful rules of dating early on.

"Hey, Stoner, how's it going?"

"*Mel*-a-nie. How's my favorite girl?"

Her shoulders thumped back against the dressing-room wall as if her leg bones had melted. She was so happy to hear from him she wouldn't even remind him—again—that she was no longer a girl. "I'm fine. Shopping with my mom and sister."

"Find anything?"

"Mmm, yes."

"Whoa-*ho,* that sounds promising. Is this an outfit I can see?"

She pushed herself off from the wall. "Well…sure. I don't see why not."

"Tonight?"

Melanie took the phone from her ear, pumped her fist in victory. *Yesss!* "Uh, tonight…hmm. Well…I guess I could be free after ten."

She was free now, but this way it sounded as if she already had plans she wouldn't change for him. As an added bonus, seeing him late would guarantee they get to the fun part of the night very soon.

"I have a gig in Waukesha. I was thinking maybe an early drink."

"Oh." *Crap.* She'd lied her way out of a date. "How early?"

"Eight?"

Now what? She should say no, make herself unavailable, as she'd already implied she was. Changing plans for a guy? No-no-no. But he was in town for only a couple more weeks and she so desperately wanted to see him. Maybe Stoner wouldn't mind a little eagerness after that amazing night. "I might be able to swing that, yeah."

"Cool. How about at your favorite, The Wicked Hop?"

"Okay, I'll try to make it."

She hung up the phone, feeling slightly disgusted with herself for caving, then grinned at the mirror again. So? She had what she wanted, a date with destiny and a great outfit to put on.

If her luck held, Stoner would have nothing better to do after his gig than take every stitch of it all the way off.

EXACTLY EIGHT O'CLOCK. Melanie stayed in her car, peering at the bar entrance. For *once,* for once she was on time—and she didn't want to be. Preparations for her date had gone at the speed of light. She'd known exactly what she was going to wear, which cut at least forty-five minutes. Then, once downstairs, she couldn't stand being around her mother's silent disapproval. Mom hadn't even *met* Stoner. How she'd figured out he was "wrong" for her was beyond Melanie. In any case, she was over her family trying to talk her out of what she had to do. Alana, Mom, Gran and Grandad—did they think she was just flitting around from one feel-good moment to the next without giving her actions any thought whatsoever?

Apparently.

Well, guess what, she'd given her own life a lot of thought, thank you very much, and had come to a rational and mature realization. She couldn't change her character before she was ready to, and she wasn't ready to. So…she could sit around beating herself up, wishing she was different, or she could enjoy life, accepting the consequences of her choices.

Seemed like a no-brainer to her.

Gran and Grandad, Alana and Tricia wanted Melanie to be someone else. For some reason she hadn't been able to make them understand it was like trying to convince an apple to be an orange, or a mosquito to be a fly. Or a Melanie to be an Alana. Ahem.

She glanced at her watch again. One minute after eight. She should wait at least fifteen minutes before…

Aw, to hell with it. Bouncing out of her car, she hurried down the sidewalk to the bar entrance, pushed her way in and eagerly scanned the interior.

There. There he was. Stoner. God, he was sexy. So masculine, so handsome, all in black again—did he own clothes in other colors? Fine by her if he didn't. Everyone knew dark colors attracted heat, and Melanie was heat personified.

She hurried forward and stopped short when Stoner leaned to his left to speak to someone. Someone unmistakable, even though all she could see was the back of his head.

Edgar.

Oh, my God.

Her reaction surprised her almost as much as seeing him.

Okay, regroup. It was fine that he was here. Really. Fine.

It just didn't feel fine, and she wasn't sure why. Maybe because of that weird joke he'd pulled in the office. Maybe Tricia's odd conviction that Melanie was in love with him.

Arghh. She couldn't stand being anything but happy around Edgar. He was such a bright spot in her life, a good friend amid the parade of changing lovers. If her mom's misguided theory ruined their close friendship, Tricia would have a lot more to pay for than destroying Melanie's childhood.

So. Edgar was here on her date with Stoner. Okay.

She continued her purposeful stride forward—as purposeful as she could manage through the bodies. Edgar wouldn't stay long. He liked his bars as quiet as libraries.

"Hi, there." She smiled warmly at Stoner.

"*Mel*-an-ie." He gave her outfit a searing once-over with those hot blue eyes. "Baby, you are looking fine."

"Thanks, Stoner." She nodded to Edgar, for the first time ever wishing he wasn't around, because she wanted to kiss Stoner's sexy lips more than she wanted to go on breathing. He was *the most* incredible kisser. "Edgar, what a surprise. This isn't your type of place."

He shook his head, looking more miserable than she would have expected. It wasn't even that crowded yet. Ten o'clock and patrons would be elbow to elbow. "Stoner convinced me to come out with him. I didn't realize...that you..."

He didn't know she was coming? Would that have made a

difference? She glanced at Stoner, wondering why he hadn't told his brother this was their date, but his eyes were wandering, his finger tapping on their table in time to the pumping music.

"I hope you don't mind that I'm here, Edgar?"

If he did, part of her would die. She would never want to have to choose between Stoner and Edgar. She couldn't.

"*No.* No. It's fine. It's great."

He did mind. This was awful. She needed to make him comfortable, show him the three of them could work even if it was weird for him at first that she and Stoner were together. If the way Stoner had checked her out was anything to go by, there would be plenty of time for kissing later on. She'd stay away from him now. Though frankly, she wanted to put her hands all over and all under black cotton and leather and send them both to heaven.

"I'll get you a drink, Mel." Edgar tried to flag a passing waitress, who ignored him.

"Thanks, Edgar."

"Excuse me!" He called to another woman with a tray, who also ignored him.

"Nah, little bro, this round's on me. What'll you have, Melanie?"

"How about a cosmopolitan?" She beamed at Stoner, noticing Edgar scowling in her peripheral vision. For heaven's sake, she couldn't even smile at her own lover?

"And another beer for me. Edgar, what's that…thing you're drinking?"

"Courvoisier XO Imperial."

"Got it. Yo', right here, darling.'" He beckoned with one finger to a stunning redheaded waitress way across the room, who immediately made a beeline for him. Edgar's scowl grew darker. Did these two compete?

Worse and worse.

"What'll you have, sweetie?" The waitress stood too close

to Stoner, offering a sexy smile and a view of her cleavage, which he seemed to be enjoying.

Men.

"Refill for me, another fancy-pants brandy for my brother here, and the lady will have your very best cosmo, straight up."

"I'll get right on that." She gave him the barest suggestion of a pouting air kiss and headed for the bar.

"This is shaping up to be an excellent weekend." Stoner winked at Melanie, which made her forgive him the boob-peeking, and slapped Edgar on the back. "You guys should come hear me play tonight."

"Thanks, not me." Edgar looked pained.

"Edgar, Edgar, Edgar." Stoner shook his head. "Dude."

"It's not his scene, Stoner." Melanie was annoyed on Edgar's behalf. He was into what he was into. Stoner shouldn't be berating him for that. She sure knew what that felt like. "I'll come, though."

"I thought you were going out with girlfriends."

Oops. She forgot she was "busy." Who could she ask for a last-minute date on a Saturday night? None of her regular crowd would be at home with nothing to do. Alana wouldn't be caught dead at any bar that would hire Stoner's band. Damn. Maybe she'd swallow what was left of her pride and sneak in by herself, see if she and Stoner could spend some more bed-rumpling time. "Yeah, we'll catch the last set, maybe."

"That'd be excellent." He grinned and her blood ran hotter. He was right. This would be a really good weekend. She was ravenous for a repeat, to reassure herself she hadn't imagined any of the deep emotions they'd shared Thursday night. Because honestly, seeing him here now wasn't exactly...

Well, he was very hot, but...

She didn't quite feel...

Stop! She wasn't going to start doubting the best thing that had ever happened to her.

"Stoner, where does your music take you next?" She couldn't bear to think that he'd be leaving. Ever.

"Indiana, then to Cleveland, Harrisburg, and on east to Connecticut before we start heading south—Carolinas, Georgia, maybe Florida."

"Wow, lots of traveling." She wasn't sure she would like that life. Maybe if they got serious he'd agree to settle down for her.

"Yeah, lots of traveling." He continued to look around the bar, drumming incessantly on the table. She would have preferred he be unable to take his eyes off her. At least Edgar seemed to be paying attention. She'd bend over to flaunt her cleavage for Stoner, which usually trapped any pair of eyes fueled by testosterone, but she didn't want him comparing her to the considerably better endowed waitress.

"You must love what you do enough to make all that wandering worth it."

"Worth it? You kidding me? I love the road. Damn, it's the life. New places, new faces, wine, women and song, you know? What's not to love?"

Melanie started feeling a little sick. That didn't sound like the words of a man ready to settle down, even for her. And she didn't like the plural "women."

"Ugh." Edgar made a face. "I'd rather be chained to a rock with vultures eating my liver."

"Dude, that is nasty." Stoner grimaced. "Man, the stuff you come up with."

Melanie blinked. She wasn't exactly an intellectual, but even she recognized the mythological reference. "That was the Greek gods' punishment for Prometheus, who gave fire to humans."

"Oh, yeah." Stoner nodded vigorously, obviously embarrassed. "I knew that. I did."

"Here we go." The waitress put down their drinks and winked alluringly at Stoner. Melanie grabbed her cosmopolitan and toasted Stoner, then Edgar, before taking a large gulp. This outing wasn't what she had expected. The dynamic was very, very weird. She'd always been comfortable around Edgar. And Stoner...well they should be acknowledging *something* about what had gone on the other night, shouldn't they? Playing footsie under the table, unable to tear their eyes off each other? Something? Shouldn't she be feeling at least a vestige of that incredibly powerful emotion around him? All she felt was her usual lust.

"Cheers." Stoner tipped his beer glass up and emptied half of it down his throat. "Ahhh, good stuff. Edgar, my man, what's new in the fencing world?"

"Not much this time of year. Competition heats up again in the fall."

"You watch fencing?" Melanie turned to Edgar. "I didn't know that. I didn't even know it was broadcasted."

Stoner laughed as if that was the funniest thing he'd ever heard. Melanie started to wonder how many beers he'd had. "Babe, he doesn't watch fencing, he *is* fencing. Champion of our high school. Wisconsin Division champion. He never told you?"

She gave Edgar an incredulous look. "Why didn't you?'

"Dude!" Stoner slammed his fist on the table. "Where are your balls? Impress the lady, for God's sake. Hell, it even impresses me."

Edgar shrugged, looking down at his drink. "Didn't think it would interest you, Mel."

"Edgar!" She cried out in pained protest and had to lower her voice. "I'm your best friend. I want to know everything about you."

"Well, now you know." He looked up then, his blue eyes, so like Stoner's, almost defiant. She felt a funny jolt when he made the contact, and had to look away.

"What else aren't you telling me?"

"He's a cross-dresser." Stoner nudged Edgar with his elbow. "Black lace panties and antique corsets and lace-up boots with stiletto—"

"*Stop.* It's not funny."

Both men turned in surprise. Melanie would have turned to herself in surprise, too, if she'd been physically able to. Where had that come from? A wave of annoyance at this guy who was supposed to be the love of her life? She just couldn't connect the man here tonight with the tender passionate hero of the darkness. It made no sense.

If Edgar hadn't admitted he was kidding about it being him in bed with her that night…

No. She couldn't think about that anymore. It was just too… she didn't know. Threatening. No, not that. Sort of…wrong.

"Sorry, Ed." Stoner narrowed his eyes thoughtfully at Melanie, as if he was expending major brain power calculating something. "I was out of line."

"S'okay." Edgar threw her a speculative look, too.

She was getting really sick of people trying to figure her out without her permission. "When you're not traveling, Stoner, what do you do for fun?"

"Oh, well, I'm really into World of Warcraft. Amazing game. I could spend the rest of my life in that world." He finished his beer and wiped his mouth. "I like to hang with friends, watch football, basketball. Rock out on guitar, of course. Oh, and movies. I'm a big movie buff."

"Cool." Melanie grinned hopefully. She wasn't much into computer gaming or football, but movies she could relate to. "Edgar and I just saw *Charlie Bartlett*. I thought it was really fresh and fun. Did you see that? About the rich kid who sells pharmaceuticals and therapy to his high school classmates?"

"Hmm." Stoner scratched contemplatively under his chin.

"Missed that one. Did you see *Saw 5?* I just rented that again. Great movie."

"*Saw 5?*" She frowned. "Never heard of it."

"Fifth in the *Saw* series."

Melanie's eyes shot wide. "Fifth? As in there were also *Saws 1, 2, 3* and *4* and I never heard of any of them?"

"You should be glad," Edgar said.

"Babe, where have you been? Greatest slasher films ever made. There's this scene in *Saw 5* where this guy has his head in a box, and the box starts filling up with water. He has to give himself a tracheotomy. Man, that was so intense. Cutting into your own throat like that? Killer."

"Ew." Melanie couldn't think of any other fitting comment.

"At the end the only two survivors of this whole gang have to fill buckets with blood, but since their friends aren't there anymore to help, they have to cut off their own..."

Melanie tuned him out, drowned herself, without benefit of a tracheotomy, in her cosmopolitan. Who was this guy? How could he be so different today than he'd been that night in Edgar's apartment? So devoid of sweetness or sensitivity? This made no sense.

There was only one solution she could think of, only one way of figuring out what Stoner had in common with her perfect lover.

And that was to get him in bed again as soon as she possibly could.

5

TRICIA SAT MOTIONLESS on the floor of her childhood bedroom, now the guest room in a house that belonged to her daughters, in the half-lotus position, palms up on her knees, thumbs and forefingers in chin mudra—forming a circuit so her body's energy could flow down to the tip of her fingers and circle back up her arms. The hand position also represented the rising of the higher mind over material and bodily concerns—forefinger over thumb.

She'd been meditating for half an hour, but her usual quick descent into peacefulness hadn't come easily today. Melanie was out with this Stoner person tonight, and Tricia's instincts were flashing warnings. The description of Stoner provided by Alana that morning while Melanie had been in the dressing room didn't help.

The only thing Tricia couldn't fit into Melanie's pattern of chasing bad boys—one Tricia understood all too well—was how she had behaved when she'd come home from spending the night with Stoner. She'd acted like a woman truly in love, but nothing about Stoner seemed to inspire such depth of emotion. Tricia knew that great sex could count for a lot of fluttery excitement. But not love.

She pushed the conscious thoughts out of her head, leaving

herself open to her inner voice, which never failed her. If only she'd discovered meditation during what she now called her wasted years. So many people put so much energy into ignoring those internal nudges pointing them to the truth. Tricia had not only ignored them, but unfailingly chosen to act in direct opposition.

Swaying gently, she sank further into her trance.

Help her.

The voice was adamant. Tricia's conscious instincts had been correct. Melanie needed her help.

She waited expectantly, calm, head clear, full of the joyful peace she never found any other way.

Unfortunately, the voice wasn't going to tell her how.

Body heavy and relaxed, she opened her eyes and let herself come slowly to the present, aware of the carpet under her, the rose-colored bedspreads over the twin beds, her easel set up in the corner, the Impressionist prints on the walls. When she was a girl, those walls had been a collage of pictures and posters cut from teen magazines or mailed from fan clubs—David Cassidy, Randolph Mantooth from the TV show *Emergency!,* Richard Hatch from the first *Battlestar Galactica* series, Alan Alda from *M*A*S*H*. Always men. She so wished she hadn't passed that obsession along. At least Alana had escaped it.

Enough. Tricia had decided that her life would not be about regretting the past, but about looking forward to her remaining decades, building a life she could be proud of when she came to its end.

She got up, wincing slightly when her knees took a few seconds to un-stiff themselves. She was in decent shape, had started working out when she went clean, but some things about aging you just couldn't fight. After shaking out her legs one at a time, she stretched her arms up to the ceiling, wondering how to help her younger daughter.

According to Melanie, she'd already tried to love a "nice

guy" when she'd invited her friend Sawyer to be her room-
mate, but Alana had shown up right when he'd moved in—
apparently straight into Alana's bed. "By mistake," Alana
had insisted. Tricia smiled and moved to the back window,
gazing at the stately elm in the yard. There were no mistakes.
Fate had brought Alana and Sawyer together, just as fate had
brought Tricia home when her younger daughter needed her
most.

Melanie did need a "nice guy" to ease her away from Stoner
and his type. Tricia would help her find the right man.

Somehow.

Since she hadn't lived in Milwaukee for decades and wasn't
keen on looking up people who knew her then, Tricia wasn't
going to be much help introducing Melanie around. However,
the Internet was full of dating sites. She could go online and
find a decent, responsible man with a regular job and a real
name. Or several decent responsible men, so Melanie could
choose.

Onward. Tricia went next door into Melanie's room, smiling at the chaos that so reminded her of the state of her own
childhood bedroom. Clothes here, jewelry there, firefighter
calendar on the wall, the Betty Boop clock and telephone that
Tricia had sent for Melanie's tenth birthday—even though
Melanie had no idea who Betty Boop was back then.

At Melanie's desk, she powered up her daughter's laptop
after removing a stack of *People* and *Vogue* magazines from
the chair so she could sit. Maybe she would have done better
by the girls if she'd surrendered them earlier to their gran and
grandad. Maybe she should have taken her parents up on their
offer to move in here so they could supervise both the girls
and their own mess of a daughter.

Tricia lowered her chin glumly onto her palm. No regrets?
Yeah, but being back home made it pretty hard not to speculate
on all the "what ifs." Still, Melanie and Alana were beautiful,
vibrant, intelligent young women in spite of having had Tricia

Surprise Me...

for a mother. Alana had found real love with a wonderful man. After Tricia helped Melanie do the same, she could move on to Florida for her next stage of making amends—being there for her parents in their old age.

Computer warmed and ready for action, she found some dating sites on Google and checked out a bunch of them. Most were expensive, a few of the free ones didn't seem to have many people signed up, another couple featured a small percentage of men seriously looking for relationships and a large percentage seriously looking for sex. Including one guy whose main profile photo was a close-up of his crotch in a G-string.

Charming.

When she found Milwaukeedates.com, Tricia knew she'd hit pay dirt. Nice-looking guys and a good selection. All she had to do was type in her search criteria. Minimum age: twenty-four. Maximum age: thirty-four. A neat ten-year span. Education: graduate of a four-year college, so he'd be on Melanie's level. Nonsmoking. English speaking. Photo required with profile. Living within twenty miles of their zip code.

A list popped up in seconds; Tricia started giggling. Shopping for men! This was a hoot.

An hour later, she had compiled a short list after carefully examining each man's introduction, keeping those who were decently articulate, preferably with a sense of humor, discarding paunchy cavemen atop Harleys, men in eye-hiding dark glasses, anyone with cliché-ridden profiles: "Know how to treat a lady right" and "Love long walks on the beach" and "I'm looking for that special someone." Honestly. Was there some dating-site phrase book they all used? What happened to originality?

Though she supposed the women's ads were no better.

List made, noting each profile's username so Melanie could check them out later, Tricia paused.

Were there men her age on the site?

She wasn't looking; she'd promised herself no dating while she was here in Milwaukee with the girls, and only in Florida well after she'd gotten herself settled and the air cleared between herself and her parents.

All the same she was curious what mainstream dating looked like for women her age. Here in Milwaukee she'd known everyone in the party set, including Jake, the guy she'd followed to Berkeley to get out of town. After that relationship collapsed, she'd met men at parties, at bars and/or clubs, through dubious friends…she cringed just remembering. Amazing she still had her health. Amazing she was still alive. No career, no retirement savings. But alive.

Minimum age: forty-eight. Some women might go for boy toys, but Tricia liked them closer to her stage of life. Maximum age: fifty-eight. Education: college not necessary. She'd never been, so why would she require that of the guy? Smoking, no way. She'd quit, didn't need that temptation. Better they didn't drink, too, though she craved alcohol much less frequently than nicotine. Within ten miles of their zip code.

When her own personalized list appeared, Tricia scanned the first page of photos, oddly nervous. A few weren't bad. One was appealing enough that she checked out his profile. Seemed like a decent guy. Maybe when she was ready to date this would be the way to go.

She clicked to the second page of photos and froze.

No. Way.

Absolutely no way.

Yet there he was—she recognized him immediately even without his beard, though he still had the ponytail.

Jim Bronson. Melanie and Alana's father's best friend, who'd been as wild as Tom in most every way, except underneath he had a solid sensitive core that Tom lacked. Naturally, then, she had fallen madly in love with Tom, though as his treatment of her worsened, she'd found herself once in a while looking wistfully at Jim, wondering why she'd made such a stupid choice. Ironic that now she was looking wistfully at his picture, wondering why she'd gone on to make so many more.

Here he was, still in Milwaukee. Single, apparently. Posing with his Harley, familiar phoenix tattoo visible on his left bicep. He looked good. Healthy. Strong. Clear-eyed. Graying hair and a few extra pounds like her, otherwise the same.

A memory came—of her, Tom and Jim wasted after some party, lying in the back of Jim's old VW van, inexplicably named Frieda. Tom had tried to interest Jim in "doing her" while he watched. She remembered being appalled that Tom thought he had any right to pimp her. And also...well, she remembered holding her breath, waiting for Jim's reaction. He'd seemed to sober up immediately, raising himself up on one elbow over them. Tricia had never forgotten the hungry look he'd given her. Nor would she forget in the next instant the look of scorn directed at Tom. And there went that plan.

A wave of emotion rushed over her, a complicated mix of nostalgia and recoil. She wanted to talk to him, to relive the old days, maybe make some sense of them. She also wanted to run and hide, bury those memories deep where they belonged, forget they ever existed.

Jim.

She hit the back button away from his profile to the original list of thumbnail pictures. A symbol appeared next to Jim's member name. *Online now.*

Just like that, she could reach through cyberspace and reconnect. As a friend, of course, an old friend. Maybe seeing him would help put some of her past to rest. Maybe through him she could find a way back to her daughters. He'd lived through her first wild days with her; he might have insights she could use to communicate some of the whys of her choices to Melanie and Alana. Maybe she could even get up the nerve to tell them more about their father.

There were no accidents. If she'd come across Jim's profile

tonight, it meant Tricia was supposed to contact him. She'd have to set up a profile on Milwaukeedates.com before she could, but that was hardly an impasse.

As quickly as she could, she filled in minimal information, pulled up an e-mail on the site, typed in Jim's username, Fotoman, then sat at a loss.

What would she say?

Hi, Jim. It's Tricia, back in Milwaukee for a while.

Spare, but anything else she thought of sounded awkward or overeager or went on too long. She jabbed the send button and collapsed back in the chair, feeling as if she'd set something huge and irreversible in motion, and not sure why. Jim was a friend. Tricia was writing to say hi. Nothing about that would scandalize her children, nothing about that would betray who she had finally managed to become, nothing about that would involve changing her plans or—

TRICIA!!!!

The e-mail leaped onto her screen, and a cold place in her heart she didn't even know was there started to thaw. She'd made friends in California, most based on the partying they shared, but some true friends, like Dahlia, who'd taken her in when her life collapsed this latest and last time. But Jim had been there from her childhood, through high school, when they'd started together down the slippery slope of delinquency, inseparable friends until Tom left her. Eight years later, she'd surrendered the girls to her parents and fled to California, unable to face what she'd done, but not at the bottom yet. That took her another fifteen years to reach.

Wasted, wasted years.

414-555-2967. Call me!

The second e-mail popped up on the screen and made Tricia jump.

Call him? She put a hand over her mouth. What had she expected, that she could contact an old friend and then not talk to him?

Betty Boop was within five feet of her, posing next to her phone in her bright red dress with pouty allure. All Tricia had to do was get up from the chair, take three steps toward Melanie's bed, pick up the receiver and dial.

She felt like a girl in junior high, terrified to call a boy she had a crush on.

But this was Jim!

Get up. Check. Three steps. Check. Pick up receiver… dial…

"Tricia."

She grinned at the sound of his voice, deeper and gruffer than she remembered, but then a lot of time had gone by. Twenty-five years. After Tom had left her, she hadn't wanted to be around anyone that reminded her of him, especially because all their mutual friends had assumed Jim would be next in her dating lineup. For sanity's sake, she'd frozen Jim out of her life and out of her heart, too.

No regrets, right? Sometimes that rule was harder to keep to than others. "Hi, Jim."

"You could have knocked me over with a dust bunny. I didn't think I'd ever hear from you again."

She was still grinning. "I always resurface. Like a bad cork."

He chuckled. "It's damn good to hear your voice, Tricia."

"Yours, too." The simple words seemed unbearably intimate. Maybe it was experiencing warm memories in her shadowed old bedroom, or calling him late on a humid, fragrant summer night; maybe it was too many months alone, but all the feelings she'd stuffed down when she knew him started resurfacing.

"You in town for long?"

"Several months. I'm here to try and make peace with my girls for being the worst mother ever."

"You gave up your children for their sakes. The worst mother wouldn't have had the guts to do that."

How did he know? She wasn't speaking to him then. "Okay, second worst."

He laughed. He'd always laughed easily—even when he wasn't stoned. "We'll have a lot of time to spend together while you're here?"

Her heart sped up. "Sure. I'll have to get a job, but... yes."

"I've thought of you a lot over the years, Tee. I kept track of you for a while through Katie until she left town, too." His voice was gentle. He'd always had an easier time expressing emotion than Tom. "After you were gone I almost picked up the phone to call your parents a dozen times, trying to find you."

"But didn't."

"I had reasons. For one, I wasn't sure how glad you'd be to hear from me."

"I'm not sure, either. I was a mess for a long time."

"Same here." He sighed heavily. "Though I've been dry and straight going on ten years now."

"Ten years." She felt deeply ashamed it had taken her so long. "A lot less than that for me. More like one."

"That's one more than people who are never able to punt the habit."

She smiled. "I suppose. I still feel like I could go around apologizing for the rest of my life to everyone I ever knew and it wouldn't be enough. Especially my girls."

Her voice broke. She hadn't been able to talk about this with anyone other than her therapist. Her parents had been good role models, but for whatever reason, she'd been born with an insatiable craving for attention—even negative attention—and excitement. Her therapist thought Edith and Edwin's undisputable virtues had something to do with it. Neither drank, smoked, swore, spoke ill of others. Both attended church, did community service—the good-person pressure was enough to make a daredevil only child go nuts.

It didn't help that there were millions of kids who would kill for the upbringing she'd so callously rejected.

No regrets.

"Meet me on Monday and I'll absolve you of your sins in a mysterious and sacred New Age cleansing ceremony."

She wrinkled her nose. "New Age who what?"

"It involves good food, good conversation and maybe a long walk if it isn't too hot."

"That sounds more like a lunch date."

"That's exactly what it is. Are you free?"

She sank onto Melanie's bed. Her first date clean and sober. Well, not *date* date, just a friendly get-together. "I'm free."

"Noon at Beans and Barley. You remember where it is?"

"Of course."

"I'll meet you there at noon."

Grinning, Tricia hung up the phone. Remarkable to be able to see someone she'd known so well in one incarnation, after being reborn into a new skin, a new chance, a new life.

Three hours later, midnight, she was sitting up in bed, staring at a painting for her best-yet idea for a kids' book—about a naughty witch who stole all the holidays from the calendar, and the brother and sister who convinced her to give them back. Tricia wasn't in the mood to work as she often did when she couldn't sleep. Her mind wasn't focused enough; it was doing cartwheels somewhere in outer space.

She should have waited until morning to contact Jim. Insomnia had become a problem even when life was calm, a by-product of stopping the self-medicating long enough to get back in touch with herself. Her therapist in California assured her once she'd slain all her family demons, sleep would return. In the meantime she'd made friends with exhaustion.

Finally giving in to the urge to be up and around, she went downstairs, made herself a cup of lavender tea to try to relax, practicing her deep yoga breathing at the kitchen counter, making her eyelids heavy, her body heavy, concentrating on the warm fragrant liquid, imagining it filling her body with—

Bang, bang, bang. Tricia jumped a mile, sloshing hot tea into her lap. Who was pounding on the back door at midnight on a Satur—?

"Melanie. You there?"

Tricia closed her eyes in exasperation. Oh, super. One of Melanie's wackos come to claim her for an evening's entertainment.

She went to the back, peeked through the storm door; her mouth formed an O of surprise. Who... This couldn't be...

Psychic intuition hit.

This was Edgar.

Bang, bang, bang.

So the man had passion. Good. She parted the curtain so he could see her, and put her finger to her lips. She wasn't going to open until she was sure it was he, and not some guy high on something that could make him violent. She'd had plenty of experiences in that department. Fine by her never to have another.

He raised his eyes—which were very blue and oddly beautiful—and caught sight of her. His fist froze in midair, then his five fingers flew open in surrender, his expression turned to sheepish dismay.

Yup. Edgar.

She unlocked the door, pulled it open. "Hi, Edgar. I'm Tricia, Melanie's mom."

She held out her hand, which he pulled himself together

enough to shake. Tricia liked him right away. His grip was
warm and firm, and in spite of the fact that he seemed over-
wrought, and had obviously been startled by her appearance,
he managed a polite smile, which transformed his face further.
Something very, very appealing about that face. Though the
hair...

"I'm *so* sorry, Mrs.—"

"Tricia."

"Mrs. Tricia. I forgot you were back. I was—" He clamped
his lips shut, looking desperate for a second, then resolved. "Is
Melanie here? She's not answering her cell. She's out with...
I'm afraid she... I don't want her to..."

"Why don't you come in, Edgar? I'm having lavender tea.
Maybe you'd like some to calm down. Melanie isn't here, but
I'm sure she'll be back soon."

"Thanks. Yes. Okay."

She let him into the kitchen, noticed him looking around
curiously. "You haven't been here before?"

"Oh. No. Melanie and I mostly see each other at work."

"Well, welcome to her home. I'm sure you'll be seeing a
lot more of the place." Tricia couldn't be surer. What a waste
of time looking online—except for finding Jim. This was the
man for Melanie. As soon as she did something about his hair.
"I take it you're worried about her?"

"Oh. Um." He rubbed his forehead wearily. Under the horrible helmet hair it was smooth and high. "She's out with my
brother, and—"

"Stoner."

"Yes. Stoner. He's playing a gig. She was going to see
him, but then they didn't come back, um, to my place...." He
blushed, looking supremely tortured by his confession. "So,
uh..."

"Have a seat, Edgar." Tricia filled the kettle, put it on the
stove. "You thought she might bring him here?"

"God." He slumped onto a counter stool. "I probably seem crazy to you."

"No more than any man in love with a woman who can't see it."

Edgar's mouth dropped about four inches. She smiled peacefully at him and got down another mug.

"How did you know?"

"Gee, something tipped me off about the way you were completely out-of-your-mind frantic because she's out with your brother."

"Yeah. That." He laughed humorlessly. "Dead giveaway, huh."

"Love is nothing to be ashamed of." She wouldn't confess to the irony that she didn't consider any of her passions to have been love. Tom came closest, but…no. Her bar was considerably higher now. "On the contrary."

"I couldn't bear them to be together. Not after we…the other night." He let his forehead drop on his hands. "I'm not making sense to you. I'm sorry. It's complicated."

The other night? Tricia's instincts perked up as she got down the lavender. "Thursday night, by any chance?"

He looked startled. "Yeah…"

Bingo. The night Melanie came home from being with "Stoner," thinking she was in love. "She was with *you* that night."

Edgar paled. "How do you *do* that?"

"I don't know." Tricia shrugged and put dried lavender blossoms into a mesh tea ball. "Things just come."

"Does Melanie know it was me?"

Tricia's mouth curled into an immensely satisfying grin. "Deep down, undoubtedly. But she's not admitting it. Denial is a powerful force."

"Denial. Oh, God."

Tricia sat opposite him, hands itching to run through that hair and test its length. At least three inches off the sides, only slightly less on top, forget the bangs, get the wiry mass off his fine forehead, give those dynamite eyes a chance to shine. Thinning shears applied liberally, but keeping a cool, spiky-tousled look—take off too much and his nose would seem bigger. Short sideburn to emphasize the strong shape of his cheekbone and jaw. Oh, yeah.

She'd worked as a hairstylist for five years before her bad habits got her fired from too many salons and she could no longer get references to be rehired. Which turned out to be a blessing in disguise because that's when she'd started drawing and painting, skills she hadn't exercised since elementary school, where the art teacher had said she'd shown a lot of promise.

"Don't worry, Edgar." Tricia patted his hand, feeling absurdly old, then went to silence the soon-to-be-shrilling teakettle. Enough jarred nerves tonight. "If you let me help you, I think we can work this out."

"We?"

"Stoner isn't for Melanie. Everyone knows that but her, and it won't take her long, no matter what happens tonight." She poured their tea, the hope in his eyes spurring on her determination even more strongly. "If you'll trust me, and you're not above a little trickery, I have an idea I think will work."

"I don't want to hurt her."

"Of course not." Tricia smiled soothingly, trying to remember where she'd unpacked her scissor set, imagining the floor covered with poufy clumps of thick wiry curls. "But there's a big difference between hurting her and giving her the surprise of her life."

6

MELANIE RACED down the stairs to her car, threw her bag into the backseat and slammed the door. She was late for work. And cranky. Monday mornings were the pits. Especially Monday mornings after complete disaster weekends. Especially complete disaster weekends that were *supposed* to be perfect blissful weekends.

She got into her car, Honey the Honda, half expecting it not to start—*et tu, Honey?*—then grimaced apologetically when the trusty engine sprang to life. Thank goodness something was acting the way she expected. Because nothing else in her life seemed to be. Not Edgar, not Stoner and certainly not her mother.

She backed out of the driveway, nearly smacking into a neighbor's car parked across the street. Terrific. Moving forward, she went over a curb, *bump, thump,* then managed to make it to the end of Betsy Ross place, turning left as usual in spite of the sign proclaiming Right Turns Only!

Saturday night at The Wicked Hop had been weird and only got weirder. Stoner had been distracted and strange the entire time, never showing even a *hint* of the emotions they'd shared only a few nights earlier. Edgar had been morose and combative with his brother. Was he jealous? She couldn't

bear to hurt him, yet if seeing her and Stoner together was
so horrible, why had he stayed?

She whacked her steering wheel. Now look. She was wishing her best friend hadn't been around.

Yes, she was. Because then at least she would have been
alone with Stoner and could have asked him what the hell
was wrong.

The evening had only gotten worse. After Stoner left for
his gig and Edgar made excuses to get away from her, Melanie
had stayed at the bar for a lonely hour, fending off creepy men,
then gone to a couple of her other favorite places to kill time
until the Imploding Bovines' set ended, wishing she hadn't
pretended to Stoner she had somewhere else to be.

Finally she'd killed enough time and had driven all the
way to Waukesha to catch the end of the show. Good thing,
because if she'd arrived any sooner, she'd be deaf.

Granted, Stoner had been incredibly sexy, wrestling with
his guitar, but she wasn't a big fan of the noise he was generating on it.

Even worse, while he'd been glad to see her, he was just as
glad to see about a dozen other people who'd shown up to hear
him, and the evening had ended not with a romantic, private,
chemistry-filled tête-à-tête generating such lust it propelled
them into bed together within twenty minutes, but instead
with a free-for-all shot-banging, cigarette-smoking bash that
had even outlasted her keenly honed partying skills. Around
3:00 a.m. she'd dragged herself home, defeated, exhausted,
turned off by the heat and choking smoke and drinking to
the point where she'd stuck with water. Once home, she'd
discovered that Edgar had called about six times, trying to
find out where she was, and she hadn't heard her phone at
all.

Sunday she'd called him back when she got up. He'd
wanted to take her out to a movie, which would have been
ten times more fun than watching his brother whack off with

his guitar. Which made her doubly cranky at Stoner and at herself. Stranger still, Edgar had sounded different. Not like himself. And nothing like he'd been Saturday night. Sort of mysterious and very cheerful and…she wasn't sure what else.

She turned onto Highway I94, the straight shot into downtown Milwaukee. Ahead of her, brake lights lit up like Christmas lights as the traffic slowed, then stopped. Too late for rush hour unless everyone else was as enthusiastic about getting to work on time today as she was.

A few police cars and an ambulance sped by on the shoulder. Oh, no. Accident. Melanie dug her cell out of her purse and called Edgar.

"Hey, Melanie. Let me guess. You're late." He still sounded different. Manic or something.

"Accident on I94. I mean, I was late anyway, but at least I have an excuse now."

"Take your time. Boss Maniscotto has a meeting in Madison today."

"Oh, thank God." She let her head thump back on the headrest. At least something had gone right. "I'll be there as soon as I can."

"I can't wait, Melanie."

She blinked. That was odd. He'd almost sounded…flirty.

Oh, God. He hadn't decided to compete with Stoner, had he? He couldn't do anything that stupid. Not Edgar. Nothing would screw up their friendship faster, and he had to realize how precious that was.

The idea rattled her so much she forgot to keep her foot on the brake and nearly rear-ended the car in front of her.

Why was nothing simple? She'd gotten up this morning and her mother had started in on her. Before coffee. Subtly at first, about how chasing men hadn't made her happy, then saying sometimes you didn't recognize what was right in front of your nose, blah-blah-blah. If Melanie hadn't been rushing around getting ready she would have asked her just to get to the point and skip the moralizing.

What was it about her that made everyone else think they knew more about what she wanted and needed than she did? Did she give off some "help me, I'm clueless" signal?

Traffic inched forward. By this point Melanie's shoulders were hunched around her ears and her hands were white-knuckling the steering wheel. *Breathe, Melanie.* Maybe she should learn one of her mother's weird meditation tips.

Half an hour later she finally pulled into the office parking lot, grabbed her bag, locked her car and dashed inside, hoping no one in any position of authority would be there.

Nope. The lobby was empty except for Anna, and she was a good person. "Hey there, sorry I'm late, horrible accident—"

"Yeah, some fender bender. It's on the traffic report. Save it. Todd isn't around today."

"I heard." Melanie grinned sheepishly and hurried to her cubicle, just past where Edgar sat at his computer.

"Hi, Eddie, I—" She froze. Turned back. Stared.

This was not Edgar.

Except…it was.

"You…um…got a haircut."

He'd gotten more than that. A nose job? Color-enhancing contacts? Chin implants? No, impossible, not in one weekend. Wait, she'd seen him Saturday night. Definitely not in one day! Especially a Sunday. Yet how could one haircut change a man's face so much?

My God. She was so flustered she just stood there, staring. His nose was no longer a comic embellishment, but a noble part of his face, like Adrien Brody or Owen Wilson. His forehead was high, clean and masculine without its covering of wiry frizz. He had excellent cheekbones. His eyes appeared larger; tousled hair and thin sideburns gave him a funky fashionable look.

Fashionable? *Edgar?*

And then she realized what else was different. His clothes fit. And didn't clash. And they were stylish, in a classic way that both fit him and flattered his body.

He looked really, really nice.

She gulped. Sank into her chair and realized she'd tossed her bag onto it so that now her hastily assembled sandwich and chips were crushed under her butt.

"I did get a haircut." He smiled, and that dazzling smile was so familiar and yet so new in this changed face that she had to drop her eyes.

Edgar?

"Why…?"

He shrugged, and even his shrug looked prouder and straighter and more masculine. "It was time for a change."

"Yes. Well." She got up from her lunch and found herself nodding too many times. "It looks great. Really great. Terrific. Wow."

"Thanks." He grinned again.

"Hey, Melanie." Jenny appeared and put her hands possessively on the soft-looking material of Edgar's black, short-sleeved shirt shot through with thin stripes of blue that matched his eyes. "What do you think of our new office hottie?"

Edgar made a face. "Be serious."

Jenny ruffled his short hair. "You watch. Women will go nuts. That adorable Marquette student, Kaitlin, already gave him his coffee free today. Did he tell you?"

"No." Melanie shook her head numbly. "Not yet."

"And I've kept count, five women have come by your cubicle today who could just as easily have e-mailed you."

"Stop, Jenny." Edgar glanced at Melanie, who tried to look impressed though she felt as if she wanted to cry.

"Excuse me." She dug her squashed lunch out of her bag and held it up. "Gotta put this in the fridge."

Mercifully, only Brown-nose Bob Stevens was in the break room, hidden behind the *Journal-Sentinel* in the corner with his cup of coffee. Melanie put her lunch in the refrigerator and leaned against the counter, taking deep breaths.

This was crazy. She was just rattled because the weekend had been so strange and she'd counted on everything being back to the same-old, same-old this morning. That was all. If Kaitlin wanted to give Edgar his coffee free, and women in the office started making plays for him, that was all great for Edgar, and she was happy for him.

Someday she might even feel that way, too.

For now she needed to be Zen, like her mother kept telling her to be, and take everything as it came, accept it, try to be true to what she knew was right.

Never mind that her mother, in the midst of lecturing her about whatever it was, had taken a phone call from some guy she insisted was an old friend, and then floated around the house with a glassy look on her face that Melanie recognized, and which filled her with irrational fear left over from childhood, when it had been completely rational. When Mom got that look on her face it meant a man. And when Mom had a man, it meant Melanie and Alana would be on their own, emotionally and way too often literally.

This was all more than Melanie could take in at once. She needed a safe haven. Edgar had been her safe haven for the past two years, and suddenly he didn't seem that safe anymore.

Where could she go? Where could she find comfort?

Immediately the images from last Thursday, the feelings, came back. Just an hour in his arms would make all this fear recede; he'd slay all her dragons of uncertainty. She knew it. If she could just make it happen. Again.

Newspaper rustled. Bob had lowered his paper to peek at her. She must look like a complete case, leaning against the counter as if she needed it to hold her up.

She smiled and reached for a coffee mug. She hadn't even been to Starbucks this morning, she'd been that flustered. But Edgar had been to Caffe Coffee. Kaitlin was likely still mooning over his new look, and would be unable to study tonight.

God, what would Melanie do if Edgar got a girlfriend and checked out of their friendship? The thought horrified her, then the selfishness of her horror horrified her more. If he got a girlfriend she'd be very happy for him. Very.

Coffee poured into one of the mugs she insisted they keep in the break room to avoid the nasty taste and environmental hazards of Styrofoam. She lifted the foul brew in a reassuringly cheery greeting to Bob and headed to her cubicle.

She would act normal today even if it made her the only one in the universe who hadn't changed.

"You okay, Melanie?" Edgar, sweet and concerned as always, able to read her like a book. As always.

"Sure, great, Monday mornings, you know." She laughed too loudly and put her mug down, powered on her computer.

"I have something for you."

"Mmm, yeah?" Something about his cautious voice put her on tense alert again.

"Here." He slid an envelope over to her side of the cubicle and continued working on his sports catalog.

"What's this?"

"Read it and see."

"Good plan." She giggled like a crazy person and tore open the seal. Inside was a typed note.

Melanie. The other night we had together was incredible. It's been so frustrating not to be able to acknowledge what we shared in public, especially that night when my brother was around. I could hardly stand not touching you. It gets worse every time I see you.

When you go to bed tonight, leave the back door open

and your bedroom lights out. Leave a trail of flower petals leading to your door. I'll come to you at midnight.

Melanie drew in a breath so long she was surprised she
didn't fill up with air and float clear away. As if she'd willed
it into being, her safe haven with Stoner was offering itself.
Somehow he knew she needed him.

"Good news?" Edgar asked offhandedly, intent on his
screen.

"Yes." She hesitated, not sure if telling him the truth would
make him revert to his sullen self from Saturday night. But
she couldn't stop telling Edgar the truth. "Your brother wants
to meet me tonight."

"Terrific. What bar?"

"Um." She felt herself blushing. "Actually..."

"Not a bar? Do I need to vacate the premises tonight?"
He gave her a sly smile and wink that were so unexpectedly
sexy in his new look that she was momentarily distracted.

"Oh, um. No. He's coming over to my place."

"Really? Sounds like a hot date. A scorcher."

"Edgar, I'm...I mean, I thought it bothered you that your
brother and I..."

"At first. Yeah, it did. But now..." He shrugged, which drew
her eyes to his very nicely broad shoulders. "I'm fine with it.
He's not in town much longer. You should take up whatever
free time he has."

"Thank you, Edgar." She clutched the note, thinking he
was the most generous guy she knew, and wondering why his
suddenly easy acceptance of her romance with Stoner bothered her on some level. Was he going to start seeing Kaitlin?
Had he fixed himself up like this for her? Was that why he
no longer cared whether Melanie hooked up with Stoner?

That would be great. Of course it would be.

God, what was happening to her?

"I guess you'll be late again tomorrow morning, huh?"

She laughed nervously. "I hope so."

"Think you'll still be able to walk?"

"Edgar!" She pretended to be shocked, vainly suppressing a giggle. "You are one bad dude."

"That's what they all tell me." He arched an eyebrow, then went back to his project.

"You're sure you're okay with this?"

"Do I seem okay?"

"Well…" She laughed uneasily. "Yes."

"Trust me, Mel, I'm *way* okay with this."

"Good." She stopped herself from nodding too hastily. "That's good."

Everything *was* okay. She'd see Stoner tonight. Edgar was fine with that; he could even tease her. This was all good, good news. Maybe everything would straighten itself out now. Maybe her mother would meet Stoner and love him and drop her objections.

That would work. Melanie grinned at Edgar. "If it's a really good night I might need a stretcher."

"Whoa." He rolled his eyes, shaking his head. "Take video. We'll show it in the break room."

Melanie burst out laughing. "That would shake things up."

She opened a file, then realized it was the wrong one, closed it, opened her e-mail, closed that, opened another file. She couldn't remember what she was supposed to be doing next on the Carson project. This day was not going to be productive at all. All she could think about was tonight, her and Stoner, in bed the way it was that first time. Those hands, those lips, the way he—

"Uh, Melanie?"

She turned in confusion. "Huh?"

Edgar pointed. She'd opened a Word document and was leaning on the *L* key, filling the page. "Oh, duh, sorry."

"Distracted?"

"Ya think?"

"You're crazy about him, huh?" Some tension crept into his voice. So maybe he wasn't quite as thrilled as he acted. Which shouldn't please her, even this little bit.

"I don't know." She gave up even facing her computer. "Sometimes I'm sure, but then...sometimes he's not what I expected."

"You deserve someone who is good to you, Melanie." The tension was still there. "All the time. Not just once in a while."

She couldn't speak. Her throat had swollen shut with emotion. Edgar...

He turned away, fiddled with his mouse, but she got the feeling he wasn't really seeing the screen. "Out of curiosity, when was he behaving like a guy you could fall for?"

"The first night we were together. Thursday. It was..." She gestured helplessly. "Perfect."

Edgar made a strange noise, as if he'd tried to cough, sneeze, laugh and shout all at the same time. She looked at him anxiously, but he was smiling as if he'd heard the greatest news of his entire life. Melanie couldn't believe the change in his attitude. She must have imagined his previous tension.

"Eddie." She laid her hand on his arm. "I'm really glad you're happy for me. It means a lot."

"Listen, if the guy is an unbelievable miracle, an absolute god in the bedroom, who fulfills your every fantasy of what a man should be, then this is a very good thing." He flashed his dynamite grin, even more disconcerting in that newly handsome face.

"He is." She laughed and smacked his forearm gently. "All of that and more."

"Good. You know I just want you to be happy, Melanie." His voice turned low and husky; for some reason she was reluctant to look at him.

"Your brother makes me happy. At least he did that night. Really happy."

Then she did look at Edgar, because for another reason she didn't understand, she couldn't not. And then she couldn't look away, because his eyes darkened and became warm and somewhat thrilling. "Then I hope he'll make you even happier tonight."

7

"TRICIA?"

"I'm up here, Alana." Tricia took a break from frowning at her reflection in Melanie's mirror. She was having lunch with Jim and nothing she put on worked with her mood. Probably because her mood kept changing. One second she wanted to show him the years hadn't taken away her sexuality; the next second she wanted to make sure he knew this was lunch between friends and not a date; the second after that she wanted to show she'd finally matured out of her party-girl stage, but that she was still young at heart; and then and then and then…

Maybe Alana could help her decide. A good bonding moment.

"Knock, knock?"

"C'mon in," Tricia called. "The door's only closed so I can see the mirror."

"Hi." Alana poked her head around the door, then came into the room almost reluctantly, not seeming able to figure out where to stand or what to do with her hands. Tricia immediately tensed. A weird vibe was coming from her daughter. Very weird.

"Anything wrong?"

"No. No." Alana shook her head a second too long. "Just stopped by. To…talk."

"Okay." Tricia sighed inwardly. The way she said *talk* meant serious emoting ahead. Normally the idea of her eldest daughter reaching out to her would have been thrilling, but did she have to pick now? Tricia was due at lunch in less than an hour and she was plenty rattled already.

"Trying on outfits?" Alana glanced at the discarded clothes strewn on the bed. Apparently she could tell it wasn't Melanie's usual mess.

"I'm having lunch today. With a friend. An old friend." Tricia pasted on a smile, wishing she hadn't sounded defensive.

"Yeah?" Alana picked up on her nerves immediately, narrowing her eyes. The woman was smart. "Someone I know?"

"Um…no. From before Melanie was born. You were too little to remember."

"Oh." She drifted into the room, arms crossed over her chest, picked up a black miniskirt discarded because it showed too much thigh. "A guy?"

"Yes. A guy." Tricia cleared her throat, feeling as if she were the daughter, and Alana her disapproving mom. "A guy friend."

Alana's jaw set. "Well."

"What, I'm not allowed to have lunch with a friend?" She spread her hands, laughed to keep the mood light.

"Of course you are. Sorry." Alana dropped the skirt as if it were on fire. "Reflex reaction to you going to meet a man, I guess."

Tricia wasn't sure if that was supposed to be as cruel as it sounded. "Alana, I'm not—"

"Mom." Alana held up her hand. "I came over because we need to talk."

As if Tricia hadn't been trying to get her to talk for the past week? And been met at every turn with resistance? "That's what I came back for."

"I know. But I've...well, to be honest, Sawyer insisted I come over." She started the barest beginnings of a smile. "He's tired of me being all uptight and grumpy about you being here."

"Me, too."

Luckily, Alana took the comment in the right spirit; the smile turned wider. "Okay. So now what?"

Tricia sighed. This was not the greatest time. But the outfit she had on, a midcalf black knit skirt and a scoop-neck turquoise top, looked as good as anything else she'd tried on, so it would do. "So now we talk. First I need to be dressed. How do I look?"

Alana examined her carefully. "You want me to be honest?"

Tricia froze in apprehension. "Yes."

"Terrific. Younger than your age. Slender, classy, and I'd say...yes, beautiful."

Tricia burst out laughing. "Whew. Had me going there for a second. I still need earrings..."

Alana tipped her head to one side. "Gold. Something small and tasteful."

Tricia grinned. "I was thinking silver and dangling."

"Of course."

Tricia picked out a pair, twisted bars of silver that hung two inches past her lobes. "These."

"No." Alana shook her head. "Too flashy. Too formal for lunch."

Tricia put them on, studied the results. They were perfect. "I'll wear them while we talk, then we can reevaluate. Want to go downstairs and get something to drink?"

"Sure." She slipped out of the room.

One more glance in the mirror, a bracing breath, and Tricia went after her, not looking forward to this discussion, but recognizing that it was necessary. Sawyer was obviously a smart man, well up to the task of coping with Alana.

There. She'd managed one positive thought.

At the bottom of the stairs, she headed for the kitchen.

"Juice? Soda?" Alana held up a can of Diet Coke and a bottle of cran-raspberry juice. "Or water?"

"Water. The soda will make me jittery and the juice will spoil my appetite." Which was pretty much nil right now from nerves. She poured herself a glass in silence that felt brittle and threatening, sat on a counter stool, then changed her mind. This felt like a courtroom, with her the defendant, and Alana the prosecutor. "Let's go outside."

"Good plan." Alana followed her out into the summer air, cool for early August, but humid. They chose chairs opposite each other, which made Tricia feel as if she were on a job interview. Or in this case, most likely a job review. Which she'd fail.

"What does Sawyer think you need to say to me?" Given that her body was tense and nervous sweat was starting, she guessed it was not going to be pretty. She'd show up to meet Jim already wrung out emotionally.

But this was not about Jim. This was about beginning the difficult task of repairing the relationship with her daughter. Tricia remembered her vividly as a big-eyed, serious girl so hard to please, while her sister would take every opportunity to cuddle anxiously whenever Tricia was home. Which was probably more often than the girls realized. Though as her therapist told her, what mattered were feelings more than facts.

"Sawyer thinks I need to get angry at you."

Tricia nodded, sipped her water. "You probably do."

"I'm just not sure how you walk up to someone and say, 'I'm angry at you and have been for the past twenty-five years.'"

"That works." She expected it, but her daughter's painful

words still stole her breath for a second. "I guess now you tell me why."

"I think you know."

"I think I do. Your words are what's important, and your feelings."

"Since when?"

Tricia gazed up into the beautiful green leafy tops of the trees around them. *Breathe.* "That's a start. I was a terrible mother, I don't deny that."

"How could you be that terrible?" Alana's voice had changed from flat to shaking. The change was welcome, made her more human and more vulnerable, someone Tricia might be able to reach. "How could you abandon us like that so often? Spend so much time with such horrible losers? How could you do that to yourself, for that matter? Where was your pride?"

"Lost. Gone. In drugs, in neediness."

"Why?" She was pleading now, for answers Tricia didn't have. "Gran and Grandad gave you everything you needed. Love, discipline...it's not like they abused you."

Tricia nodded, throat tight, trembling, trying to stay calm and be the good parent she hadn't been before. "I learned in therapy that not everything in this life can be analyzed in neat cause-and-effect diagrams. Look at you and Melanie. Same parents, same upbringing, very different people."

Alana hunched her shoulders, then released them. "Yes. True. I'm probably just being a control freak wanting neat answers on a neat list. Even though I know life isn't like that I can't help wanting it to be."

"I get that. I do. Maybe you should try meditating or taking yoga. Both help you get into a zone of peaceful being, of accepting more about you and your life and whatever happens." Tricia hid a smile at the open skepticism on her daughter's face. "As for your anger...I don't blame you, Alana. I'm angry, too. I wasted a large portion of my life, and my relationship with the two of you. I can't fix the past, but…I can offer us the future. If I blew off the privilege of being your mother, at least I would like to try now and be your friend."

Alana looked down without responding. Not exactly heartwarming, but at least she didn't say no, which Tricia knew she was capable of doing.

"I do have one other question." She lifted her head.

"Shoot." Tricia raised her glass to her lips, feeling parched.

"Where is our father?"

Tricia put the glass down without taking a sip. "I don't have any idea, Alana."

"Tell me." Alana leaned forward, hands folded. "The truth. No matter how ugly."

Tricia sighed, wishing she'd been able to talk to Jim before this conversation. Or to her parents. Or Dahlia, or her therapist. So she could know what to tell and how.

But she was a big girl now, and this was her responsibility. No more shirking. "Tom left when I was pregnant with Melanie. He told me one day that he hadn't planned on being tied down with a family that young and that he had to find himself. He went to India on a spiritual quest. That was the last I heard of him."

Alana sat up, took a swallow of her Diet Coke. So repressed, so held in. Such a contrast to free-spirited Melanie. "Did you love him?"

"As much as I could at that age in that state. Though he didn't deserve it."

"You must have been devastated."

The comment came out of the blue, Tricia hadn't been asking for sympathy. "I was, but that's no excuse for how I treated you."

"Were we planned? He didn't make it sound like we were."

A lie came readily to her lips—how could you tell a child

she wasn't wanted? Tricia pushed it away, finished with lying. "When you have your own children you'll understand. I loved both of you the second I knew I was pregnant, and celebrated both your arrivals. It didn't matter to me that you weren't planned."

"Maybe it mattered to us."

"If you mean that your lives might have been more traditional, maybe. But I probably would have been just as bad a mother. That's the horror of addiction."

"Was he into drugs also?"

Tricia nodded sadly. "Worse than me."

"So this guy you're having lunch with knew our dad." She frowned thoughtfully when Tricia nodded. "I'd like to meet him sometime."

"I'm sure you will." Tricia blew out a long breath of relief. She wasn't sure what bomb she'd expected, but it hadn't come.

"Thanks for...talking, I guess."

"Anytime, Alana. It's what I'm here for."

Alana stood up. Tricia stood also, and after the excruciating moment when it was obvious a hug was in order, but too uncomfortable for either of them, they both laughed. That was something. If she couldn't have acceptance yet, laughter with her eldest daughter was the next best thing.

By the time Tricia was on the road to meet Jim at Beans and Barley, she was a bundle of nerves. Just how she wanted to be on a date!

No, not a date. Lunch with a friend.

Traffic was light, wind blew recklessly around the interior of her old Chevy Malibu, Louise, named after a friend who'd lived many years longer than the doctors told her she would. The car also, against all odds, was still getting Tricia places. The drive from Berkeley to Milwaukee had had her on edge, but Louise had persevered as she did today, onto I43 and up to North Avenue.

Tricia parked in the restaurant lot and hurried toward the door. Arriving late, flustered and overheated hadn't been her plan, but the Jim she knew wouldn't care.

The thought warmed her through the doors, past the small grocery area toward the restaurant, where her heart stopped. She swore it did.

Jim. Smiling at her, his gray eyes as vivid and young as ever, the gray at his temples flattering his features. She'd forgotten how tall he was, how imposing, how she felt girlish and small next to him. Tom had been five foot nine and slender. Jim was well over six feet and solid.

"Damn, Tricia, look at you." That solid body wrapped itself around her in a hug that brought tears to her eyes.

"Jim."

He didn't let go, even when he loosened his grip enough to search her face.

"You're still so beautiful. I can't tell you what this is—" He broke off, cleared his throat, and she realized with a shock that he was only just holding back his own tears. "Look at me, ready to bawl like a baby."

She was glad to be a woman; her tears were able to roll down her cheeks without shame. "It's so good to see you, Jim."

He wiped his eyes. "I feel like something I didn't realize was missing has been given back to me."

She had no idea what to say to that. His words made her feel secure, treasured and slightly bewildered.

"Well so." He released her, grinning. "I think we can just calm down and have lunch now. What do you say?"

"Sounds like a good idea."

They sat at a table by one of the tall windows looking out onto North Avenue. Tricia buried herself in the menu, overwhelmed by how familiar and strange it was to be here again with Jim. Without Tom. The place had started serving food a couple of years after they'd graduated high school. She remembered coming with her hippie friends soon after the restaurant opened, drawn to the quality vegetarian options the rest of this bratwurst-loving city hadn't offered.

Now the place was still around, and vegetarian and organic had become mainstream and trendy. Go figure.

"It's good to be here."

"The building burned down in '93, did you know that? It was rebuilt from nothing."

"Really?" She glanced up, then had to look back down at her menu. The expression on his face could be her undoing. The warmth in his eyes, the light... "I thought it looked different."

"I recommend any burrito or the tempeh Reuben. But everything's as good as you remember, or better."

The waitress appeared and Tricia ordered the Reuben, too scattered to be able to concentrate.

"I'll have the same. And iced tea." He handed his menu over, folded his hands on the table. Tricia felt naked in front of that gaze without her menu to hide behind. "So, Patricia. Tell me everything. Catch me up."

She leaned back in her chair, overwhelmed. "Oh, wow."

"I know, too big a question. Start smaller. How are Melanie and Alana? How are they liking having Mom back in town?"

She was touched he remembered their names. So long ago, so many damaged years in between. "Funny you should ask."

"Uh-oh." He quirked his eyebrow, a habit so familiar she nearly cried again. "Better tell me."

She told him, awkwardly at first, then gradually more and more coherently until she was pouring out the story, embarrassed when their food arrived and the poor guy hadn't gotten a word in.

"God, I've been blabbing forever. I'm sorry."

"I asked because I wanted to know." He reached across the table, took her hand in his large one and gave it a squeeze. "The girls need time. I had the same trouble with my nephews—hell, with everyone I knew who wasn't part of the problem in my life. Give them time, and show them by living clean that you mean it when you say you've changed. They'll come around."

"Thank you, Jim. I hope so." The rush of pleasure was almost sexual. He understood. Jim had been through it all. Talking to him today was like coming across someone of your own species after living for years among aliens.

"What are your plans?" He released her hand, started eating. "You said you were here only for a few months. You going back to California?"

"No." She took a bite of her sandwich, salty and rich—she didn't miss the meat at all. "California and I are through. I'm moving to Florida."

"Florida." He looked startled. "You are *kidding* me."

She didn't know whether to be amused or irritated. Was it that hard to believe? "No, not kidding. My parents are there."

"I've been thinking of…anyway. How are Edith and Edwin?"

"Wow." Tricia shook her head in awe. "You have an incredible memory for names."

"Only of people I care about."

She smiled, and had a hard time tearing her eyes away from his so she could remember what he'd asked, and form a response. "So far, my mom and dad are doing great. I think they're finally letting their hair down, now that they're released from raising me and then having to raise my children." She tried not to let the guilt show in her voice. "Eventually they'll need me. I thought I'd try being dependable for a change."

The warmth in his eyes showed his admiration. "You're a good woman, Tee."

The nickname made the moment too intimate; their chemistry made it too tempting. She had to become one with her sandwich or risk leaping across the table and kissing him. "I try."

"What will you do down there?"

She shrugged. "Get a job, I suppose. I started painting several years ago. I'd love to do something with that, but it's a pipe dream. Most likely I'll go back to hairstyling or waitressing."

"What kind of painting?"

"Illustrations for kids' books. I had an author I worked with in California, but she couldn't get published. Tough market."

"I have a friend here in Wisconsin who writes children's books. I can see if she knows anyone who could use you."

"Wow, Jim, thank you, that's very sweet." She smiled, touched by his offer. "Now no more talking about me. I want to know about you."

"I'm still in photography. I've made a respectable profession of it, actually. I do portraits, but also some commercial shots. Pays the bills. Hard to find time to do the more artistic stuff I love, but…"

"My daughter Alana is a photographer. She let it slide for a while, but she's doing more again. She and her boyfriend are renovating a building downtown for artists."

"I heard about that. Sawyer Kern. Big-money family here."

"Yes." She finished the first half of her sandwich and drank some water, nervous about the question she was desperate to ask. "What do you hear from Tom?"

"In Tibet. Farming yaks."

"Whoa." She tried to remain politely interested. "Is he happy?"

"You know Tom. This will last awhile, then he'll be on to something else. Before this he was in Nepal running a supply business for climbers. Before that he was in India attached to some teacher. He won't find himself if he keeps looking outside himself to do it."

She nodded, a lump in her throat, but not as big as she might have feared. "Is he clean?"

Jim pressed his lips together before he shook his head.

Tricia nodded, and felt a release she hadn't expected. He couldn't be any type of decent father to her girls. She was absolved from trying to track him down and get them acquainted.

"Miss him?"

"No." She was happy to realize it was true. "I had a fantasy of him being some kind of father to Alana and Melanie, but it's good to let that go."

Jim nodded. "I'd like to meet your girls one day, Tee."

"I'd like that, too." She felt her smile tremble, a warning sign she needed to heed.

But they talked so easily, catching up on the past few decades, on old friends, on their loves and losses, successes, failures—everything usual, but on a more honest and natural level than Tricia was used to. It made her aware of how tightly she'd held herself for so many months since her recovery, worrying about the right thing to say, so as not to give away anything about her past.

The longer they talked, the more she enjoyed herself, and the more she enjoyed herself, the more she was aware that her feelings for Jim, dormant for so many years, were threatening to explode. Sexual feelings, yes, but also admiration and a dangerous vulnerable sweetness.

"Did you want anything else?" The waitress startled them.

"No, thanks." Jim looked at his watch, shook his head and pulled out his wallet.

"What?" Tricia looked at her watch. Three o'clock! "Oh, my gosh."

"You have somewhere to be?" He handed his credit card to the waitress, watching Tricia in concern.

"No, I just…didn't realize." She laughed self-consciously. "Thank you for lunch. It was really nice to see you."

"You're welcome." He signed the receipt, kept his copy. "Let's go."

She got up, giddy and let down at the same time, wanting to stay, greedy for more of the feeling of belonging with someone, on whatever level.

Outside, he touched the small of her back, guiding her away from her car. "C'mere. I want to show you something."

Across the parking lot sat an old model Harley. She turned to him. "No way. You still have her?"

"I do." Pride rang unmistakably in his voice. "And two helmets. Want a ride for old times' sake? I have something else to show you."

She laughed, reached out and touched the scratched but still shiny chrome. "Talk about memories. Will it take long?"

"Half an hour, tops."

"How can I say no?"

"You can't." He retrieved a helmet, grinning, and climbed on the machine, a 1985 touring bike, an Electra Glide, which he had bought when he'd inherited some money from a grandparent. Tricia strapped her helmet on and climbed on behind him, assuming the familiar rider position instinctively, hands to the sides of his waist, loving the solid feel of his body. He and Tom had both owned bikes. Tom had sold his to buy his plane ticket away from his life and his responsibilities and her.

"Ready?"

"You bet." She grinned when he started the motor, grinned as they moved into traffic, grinned all the way to Brady Street, loving the ride. He pulled up to park in front of a small building. On the first floor was a sign: Jim Bronson Studios.

She climbed off the bike, took off her helmet, staring. "Look at you. This is really fabulous, Jim."

"Thanks." He took her helmet, locked it away. "This isn't what I wanted to show you."

He led her around the building, where an alley bisected the block. In back was parked...

"No way." Frieda. His old VW van. Rusty here and there, dulled, but big as life.

"Another trip down memory lane, huh?"

"I can't believe you still have her." Tricia laughed, moved forward and touched the faded blue paint.

"She's a rust heap, taking up space. I just couldn't get rid of her."

Tricia walked toward the back, hearing keys jangling behind her, wondering if he remembered that night Tom had tried to get a threesome going. What a life she'd led.

Jim unlocked the rear doors, threw them open. "Voilà."

She stood staring, ridiculously moved by the sight of the crappy old van's carpeted cargo space. They'd gone on countless trips in the thing, parked wherever, stayed up most of the night singing, drinking, sharing stories. And when they couldn't stay awake anymore, they'd slept in the back. She and Tom had probably conceived at least one of their daughters there.

Those were the days. And they also...weren't.

"Get on board." He sat, legs dangling off the back, patting the gray carpet next to him.

She climbed in, shaking her head. "It still smells the same."

"Not sure that's a compliment."

"It's just right." She turned to him, intending to smile and tell him how happy she was to be reminded of the good times as well as the bad.

But he was closer than she expected. His gray eyes, which she always expected to be cool because of their foggy, misty color, were warmer than they should have been. Her next words jammed in her throat.

"Tee." His arm came around her. Then whatever he'd been about to say must have gotten stuck, too, because he sat staring at her and she sat staring at him, and finally, maybe in desperation to break the stalemate, they both leaned in at the same time and started kissing.

Explosive. She couldn't describe it any other way. The passion didn't come on gradually, didn't mount slowly as they became familiar with each other's lips, it just poured over them like someone had Niagara Falls on a switch and turned it on.

Nothing was said, but she knew where this would go very quickly, and she sensed he knew it, too. Somewhere in the back of her mind was the understanding that sex with Jim wasn't a good idea, that there was some reason to pull away from the power of what they were experiencing together, and try to reconnect with her sanity. But with his mouth and hands on her, and hers on him, she pushed them away.

Footsteps approaching from the alley had Jim's lips and hands off her and her top tugged straight before she realized what was happening.

And when she did realize what was happening she felt a wave of nausea roll over her. What if their lovemaking had already progressed and it had been a policeman or someone who called the cops? What if she and Jim had been arrested? How could she convince her girls she'd turned over a new leaf screwing a guy on the first date in full public view?

"Jim, what did we almost do?"

"Come on, it hasn't been *that* long, has it?" He winked at her. "I don't know about you, but I'd say we're about twenty-five years overdue for some fun in the back of Frieda."

He remembered. But the knowledge didn't seem to matter now. "What if we'd been caught? What would my girls—"

"We weren't caught." He kissed her, tenderly, twice. "And next time we will be in a private room."

She didn't say yes. She didn't say no. She was still horrified at how quickly she'd thrown away all her resolve, all her good intentions.

Maybe she'd never be able to leave her past behind.

8

MELANIE LAY IN BED, waiting. Waiting some more. And then, for a change, waiting. She was not feeling the way she thought she'd be feeling as the clock ticked toward midnight. Of course, she was incredibly excited that Stoner would be here soon. But something Edgar had said resonated.

How did she deserve to be treated? Somehow in her mind, pursuing men had gotten too tied up in how she felt about them, and not enough with how they made her feel. Absence of a father figure in her early life—had that made her crave male attention, positive or negative, however she could get it? Did she want a man like Stoner, who ran hot and cold, or did she deserve something better? And why didn't she ever insist from the beginning that she be treated well? And why did women like Alana feel so differently? Was Melanie just weak?

These were not the kinds of thoughts she wanted to be having with five minutes before Stoner's scheduled arrival— though knowing him, he wouldn't be close to on time. She wanted to be lying here thinking about the great sex they were going to have, getting herself so aroused that having orgasms would be automatic. She didn't want to be edgy and distracted, and she *really* didn't want to be thinking about Edgar's new look, Edgar's new attitude, Edgar's new possible girlfriend and Edgar's new indifference to her hoped-for relationship with his brother.

Stoner. Two minutes to go; she had to think about Stoner. Concentrate on his compact, muscular body, his sexy energy, his piercing blue eyes so like Edga—

Ahem. His piercing blue eyes that drilled holes into her willpower. She had to think about the way he'd wrapped himself around her naked body as if he wanted to absorb her into his.

Mmm. She stirred in her clean white sheets, wearing black lace and nothing else, toes and fingernails painted bloodred. He wouldn't see those in the dark, but they wouldn't be in the dark all night. After they'd worn out each other's bodies, she wanted to be able to look in his eyes and judge his feelings from words and expressions, not just his very fluent sex-language.

A soft sound downstairs. She tensed, ears straining. Was that him?

Footsteps coming slowly up the stairs. Very slowly. *Step. Step.* Was he stopping to pick up the rose petals?

Step. Step. Step. Coming closer down the hall. She let out the breath she'd been holding, moved over to make sure he had room.

Her clock ticked over to midnight; at that exact moment, a soft brush against her door made it swing open. A dark male silhouette was briefly visible before the door swung shut again.

On fire. Instantly. Her body burned, her breathing grew shallow. He hadn't even touched her yet.

"Hi." She lay still, eyes straining for his shape.

"Hi." His whisper was the sexiest, most intimate sound she'd ever heard—until she heard the swish of clothing, the snap-zip of a fly, more sounds of clothing sliding over skin.

Even sexier.

Then the mattress dipped as he sat, swung his legs onto the bed and moved toward her. *"Melanie."*

She closed her eyes to process the barrage of thrills. Yes, yes, yes. This was him. This was Stoner, this was the man she'd gone head over heels with in one crazy night. All the ways he'd treated her since then didn't matter if he made her feel all those emotions again, if he'd stay and wake up with her and keep the feelings going.

His skin met hers; the familiar beautiful body surrounded her again, rough chest, muscular shoulders, long strong legs tangling with hers. She wished suddenly that she hadn't bothered with the silly lace lingerie. Why put anything between them, especially when he couldn't see? She should have saved it for later.

His hands stroked firmly up and down her back, that delicious demanding, cherishing touch that made any massage she'd ever gotten, no matter how perfectly delivered, seem cold and clinical. His mouth found the spot where her neck and shoulder met; his tongue applied warm wetness, which the room's air chilled for a second before his lips dried her. So many sensations, on her skin, in her brain, in her heart.

"I'm so glad you're here." She whispered the words, then turned to wait for his perfect mouth, exploring up her throat, across her cheek.

"Same here." He kissed her, kissed her again, varying pressure and position until she writhed against him, wanting more, but not wanting him to stop. Ever. And then suddenly, in the midst of this absolute bliss, with her lips locked on to his, she got a completely different picture in her mind.

Edgar. Winking at her at work with his new haircut, his new outfit, confident and—

God, no.

She broke away from Stoner's kiss and sat up. No. No. No. She was not going to let anything ruin this night, which she'd been dreaming about since she left him asleep last Thursday.

She needed him to drive out thoughts of anything else, of anyone else, to make her think only about him.

"Do me. Right now." If he thought she sounded desperate he could chalk it up to supreme lust. "Not nicely. Not sweetly. Not as if you like me at all."

For three long seconds he didn't move and she was afraid she'd freaked him out, that he wouldn't understand, or wouldn't be turned on by the demand. Then the mattress heaved as he got to his knees. A firm hand landed at the back of her neck, pushed her forward to her knees. A pillow was shoved under her stomach. She heard the tearing of a condom packet, the quick snap of it going on, then those strong hands gripped her hips.

"Hold still."

Sensing his warm body behind her, she waited, breathless with anticipation, vulnerable with her rear in the air, knees spread, exposed to whatever he chose to do. Her arousal climbed with her impatience.

One hand moved, then she felt his fingers stroking her firmly, her clitoris, then inside her, out again, lubricating her, turning her on, making her wriggle and push back like an animal in heat. The fingers persisted, skillful, relentless, driving her close to the brink. She was panting, quivering, nearly ready to come, and he'd barely touched her.

"Like that?"

"More. All of you."

He chuckled.

Huh? "What is so funny?"

"You." He thrust inside her with a sudden, nearly painful speed that made her cry out in pleasure-pain.

"Why...me?"

"You're such a coward, Melanie." Another thrust, as strong as the first, making her body lunge forward, her breasts swing.

He didn't sound right. Her brain dimly registered that he

didn't sound right as his cock pushed again, and again, a faster rhythm now.

"No! I'm not. I'm not." She felt feverish, trembling, waiting for the next assault, welcoming each one, denying the voice that was trying desperately to tell her the one truth she most didn't want to know about this man.

"You are scared to death."

"Of...what?"

"This. Us." He pushed again, spread her cheeks and pushed rhythmically on her anus with the pad of a finger, sending her bursts of additional pleasure.

"No. No, I'm not scared."

"What's my name?"

"Stoner."

"Tell me."

"Stoner." Why was he doing this? She didn't understand.

"Tell me." The force of his thrusts bouncing against her made her so hot she was nearly coming, on the edge, so close, out of her mind.

"Don't make me."

"Tell me." He reached under and touched her clitoris, already slippery with sex. "Say it."

"Stoner."

"No." He pumped her savagely; she went over the edge, burning up, then pulsing on and on, shoving her face into the pillow to stifle her shouts.

Sex had never ever been this hot, this good, not with anyone. Her orgasm had been huge, but her body felt unsatisfied still. Would she ever get enough of her lover-in-the-dark?

"More," she demanded.

"Right away?"

"Mmm."

"You got it." He helped her turn over, put his hands behind her knees and drew them up by her shoulders, knelt between her legs.

"Melanie."

She shook her head. "Don't talk. Just do me. Hard."

"Why, because it's safer?" He laughed, but drily. "Come on, Melanie."

"Shhh." She reached for his shoulders, pulled him down to kiss her. This couldn't be happening. This was Stoner. She wasn't going to think otherwise.

He pulled away, steadied her spread knees and sank into her again with a sigh of pleasure that nearly brought her to tears.

"Melanie." He began a gentle rhythm this time, in spite of her wanting it rough. "I'm going to turn on the light."

"No." She started to panic. The physical feelings were so delicious, why didn't he leave everything else out of it? Wasn't that enough? She didn't want to cope, didn't want to know what she was so afraid she already knew, and had probably known from the beginning. *"No.* Not yet. Please."

"I want to see you," he whispered. He kissed her forehead, her cheek, her mouth. "And I want you to see me."

Tears came, flowing from her eyes, down her cheeks. He stiffened, then relaxed. His rhythm slowed further; he stroked her hair, kissed away her tears, brought her legs down onto the mattress on either side of him, then wrapped his arms around her and lay with his cheek next to hers, sliding in and out at a slow, lovely pace that was like keeping a pot of something delicious on the stove at the perfect hot simmer.

A respite. Her panic abated. She could go on like that for hours.

"Sweetheart." He kissed her, and she slid her arms around his neck and held him like that, no longer thinking, just feeling. She let go completely, of everything but this man's beautiful way of making love.

And then when her body was totally relaxed, her libido took over again, letting her know she was ready for round two.

She lifted her hips, responding more definitely to his thrusts. He got the message, quickened his pace, now and then grinding his hips against her in a tantalizing circle.

A steady rise until she was again panting and bucking, straining harder for her second climax, feeling it within reach. He lifted up on his forearms, brought the focus of his thrusts up higher toward her clit and the climb became a certainty. A light sweat broke out on her body; she felt herself flush, felt the orgasm gathering force.

"I'm going to come." She held him tighter, repeated the phrase in a soft whisper.

He groaned and tensed; she sensed him holding back, waiting.

"Now. *Now.*" Ecstasy burned across her, more intensely than the first time, and he let go and joined her with a deep sigh.

She let herself slump back, a dead weight into the pillows and mattress, spent for now.

Perfect. Perfect.

He moved, his body straining to her left in an odd way that threatened to pull him off her entirely.

A second later she realized what was happening, too late to stop him. The light went on and forced her to confront what she must have known deep down, but wasn't able to admit, even to herself.

Edgar. Still inside her. Looking down at her warily, with his hot new haircut, his beautifully muscled arms still holding her.

Oh, God.

She wriggled away from him, yanked the sheet up to cover herself and glared, chest heaving with shock, even as her subconscious gave her a big told-you-so. "How could you do this?"

"Do what? Make love to you? Make you come twice?"

"Impersonate your brother." Her outrage made her voice

squeak. "Try to get into my pants in a totally underhanded way."

He rolled his eyes, looking annoyed with *her*. "I *told* you it was me the first time. You didn't believe me. In fact you looked as if just the thought was going to make you throw up."

"I didn't believe you because——" She stopped abruptly. Why didn't she?

"Because I am such a known liar?"

"You could have insisted."

"Maybe. But you looked so disgusted that my ego couldn't handle it."

A twinge of conscience. He hadn't understood. "I wasn't disgusted. It was just...confusing."

"It looked a lot more like revulsion than confusion to me."

She held the sheet tighter to her, searching for the upper hand. "So you wanted back in bed with me and——"

"Of *course* I wanted back in bed with you. You wanted back in bed with me, too."

"I wanted back in bed with Stoner."

Edgar rolled his eyes again. "Yeah, good luck with that. I'm sure you'd have a great time with him. Much better than what we have together."

"How do you know I wouldn't?" She shouted the words at him, even knowing he was right. Hell, she'd known the same thing about Stoner.

"Because everything in Stoner's life is about Stoner and always has been."

She closed her eyes. He was right again. But...this was still wrong.

"You shouldn't have made me think you were Stoner again tonight."

"No. I probably shouldn't have. But Melanie, I wanted the

chance to show you again how good we are together, and I knew you'd never let me into your bed any other way."

He was right. *Again*. This was becoming tediously predictable.

"But..." She tried to find some way to score a point somehow, because she was sure on some level she'd been wronged. Yet she was so hopelessly confused by this time by what she felt and thought and understood—or only thought she understood—about this man and her feelings for him that... she couldn't even think straight enough to understand what she'd just thought.

"Here's my deal, Melanie."

"Your deal? Shouldn't *I* be calling the shots right now, after you tricked me like this?"

"Nope." His grin was still his endearing Edgar grin, but his assertiveness was new. And not entirely unattractive.

Argh! She was having as hard a time reconciling this familiar friend with the wild man she'd spent the last forty-five minutes rolling around with as she had trying to reconcile dopey Stoner with her perfect lover-in-the-dark.

Would her love life ever be normal? Would she ever go on a series of pleasant dates with someone, gradually become more attracted, fall deeply in love, get married and live happily ever after?

No.

"Here's the deal," he repeated. "You go out with me three times. Three dates, real dates, not buddy dates. My location, my activity, my treat. During this time, you can date Stoner as many times as you want. After you've been out with me three times, I'll ask you again if you want to be with me romantically or just as a friend. I swear to you that I will respect your decision."

She believed him. Completely. Because up until tonight she'd trusted him completely, and even now, though she was still horrified at what he'd done, she couldn't be completely horrified, because on some level she must have known it was him all along.

"Or what?"

"Huh?" He tilted his head to one side, and she wished he'd put on clothes again because seeing Edgar naked was like… no, not exactly like seeing a brother naked, because his body was really pretty incredible, and because she knew what he could do with it.

Okay, nothing like seeing a brother naked. It was the face she couldn't handle, that dear familiar face on top of raw sex waiting to happen. It was like those pictures when people Photoshopped one head onto someone else's body.

But this was Edgar in his entirety, someone she'd been close to for two years without really knowing.

"You lied about having a girlfriend. You lied about being Stoner. Why should I believe you this time?"

He sighed wearily. "Because, Melanie. It's always been about you for me. Without my 'girlfriend' Emma, you would have been too nervous to let yourself get close to me, while as your 'buddy' safely involved with someone else, I was completely unthreatening. I was also completely unthreatening in the dark, sexually, when I was Stoner, because he's a doofus you could never be serious about.

"I want you to pull those images together and see me for who I am. I'm done being afraid where you're concerned, Melanie, not after coming this far, because I know I can make you happy. Much happier than my brother could, and *much* happier than all the losers you've been wasting time with for so long."

Right again. It's just that…he was *Edgar*. Not one of the deliciously dangerous bad boys she loved so much. Except in the dark, where he had it all over every one of them.

God, this was confusing.

"Three dates, Melanie. It's not asking much."

"No." She wrinkled her nose. "No, I guess not."

He laughed. "It's at least a step up from the guillotine."

"I know. I know, Edgar. I'm sorry, this is just..." She waved at the room, let her arm drop.

He picked up her hand and held it. She wanted to snatch it back, which he must have sensed, because his face shut down and he released her gently.

"We'll take this slowly, Melanie." He got up off the bed and started putting his clothes back on, which made her feel both sadness and relief. "As slowly as I can stand it after knowing what we can be together. I promise I'll be the perfect gentleman, and won't push you to do anything physically unless you're comfortable with it."

His beautiful body disappeared into his pants and shirt until he was once again her friend Edgar, though with clothes that matched and a great haircut that had so changed his face.

"Deal, Melanie?" He stood at the foot of her bed, hands on his hips, watching her.

She nodded, glanced up at him, dropped her eyes, then told herself not to be such a wimp and looked up again. "Just one thing."

"Mmm?" He reached down and squeezed her foot under the sheet, stroked it gently.

"Did Stoner have anything to do with tonight? I mean, were the two of you plotting to—"

"No. Absolutely not. Stoner is, as usual, clueless in all things."

She sighed. "So this was all your idea."

"Not entirely." He released her foot and took a few steps toward her door; she was disconcerted to find she wasn't ready to let him go yet.

"You had help?" God, she hoped not Kaitlin.

"The idea was mutual, but I needed a kick in the pants to make it happen."

"Who kicked you?"

He grinned, lunged suddenly across the bed and planted a sweet, tender kiss on her lips she recoiled from only slightly, and only from the surprise of it. Then he climbed off and opened the door, let himself out, and leaned back in for a second, just as she was going to remind him he hadn't answered.

"Your mother."

Her jaw dropped. He winked and started closing the door.

"Good night, Melanie." Just as the door latched, she could have sworn she heard him speak again, three more soft words, whispered into the dark hall.

"I love you."

9

EDGAR WAS HERE. Melanie wasn't dressed. She didn't want to go. She couldn't decide what to wear. She'd just tell him she was sick. No, having horrible menstrual cramps.

Her room was strewn with discarded outfits. This one was too sexy, this one he'd seen a hundred times, this one not flattering. She hadn't slept well, her eyes were puffy, her hair looked as tired as she felt.

She didn't want to go.

How many dates had she been on? Countless. She couldn't recall ever being this nervous, this scattered, this convinced everything about the evening would be a disaster.

What could she do? If she canceled tonight, he'd reschedule. Three dates. Tonight's misery times three.

Worse, she'd called Stoner to schedule a date with him, and he hadn't returned her call.

Terrific. The guy she wanted wasn't interested except when he happened to be around her, and the guy she wasn't interested in was all over her.

"Melanie!" Mom calling from downstairs. *"Your date's here."*

Yes, Mom, I know. "Be down in a second!"

Two seconds. How many seconds? She had to wear something. Going downstairs in her underwear would certainly send the wrong message.

Damn it. *Damn it.*

Fine. Whatever. She grabbed a pink skirt, tight through the hips, then flaring down a few inches above her knees. It was reasonably ironed; she'd wear that. Fine. She dragged it on, adjusted quickly, zipped. With it…

There. She pounced on a white tank top discarded earlier for being too low-cut. Tough. At this point she'd wear whatever, and who cared anymore. She sure as hell didn't. She wanted this evening, this date, over with as soon as possible. Maybe she could break out in a nice case of measles. Or food poisoning.

God, a date with Edgar, how did she get herself into this mess?

She jammed on tan strappy sandals that climbed up her ankles, and glanced in the full-length mirror hung on the back of her bedroom door. Well. She looked okay for a disaster. He'd think so, anyway. That was Edgar, always complimentary. She always felt pretty and desirable when she was with him. Even when she hadn't been aware of the extent to which he, um, desired her.

Melanie screwed her eyes shut, fisting her hands. She couldn't deal with it. Nor her extraordinary response to him in the dark. No, no, no. Not Edgar. No. Nothing would happen tonight or the other two nights. Nada, zip, *niente.* Then she and he would put this behind them and settle back into platonic friendship, and everything would be fine again.

That settled, she checked her makeup for only the third or fourth time, decided her lipstick was too plummy, and painted over it with a layer of pink that blended just right to match the skirt.

Okay? Hmm. Mascara a little clumpy on her left—

Argh! What was she doing all this primping for? This was

Edgar. *Edgar.* He wouldn't care if she wore a garbage bag with armholes.

She was ready.

Except for not being ready.

One, two, three, go. She opened the door and stood there. It took another count of three to get her to move her feet out into the hallway, down the hall, to the top of the stairs, where she could hear her traitor mother and Edgar talking and laughing. He could charm anyone. Everyone liked Edgar. When she got home tonight, her mom would be waiting up and would give her a special smile and a wink and say, "What a nice man" and do everything she could to make sure Melanie married him before she went to Florida.

Argh!

One, two...no, wait, she'd done that. Three, four...nope, done that, too. Six, seven, eight, nine—

"Melanie!" Her mother, sounding impatient, Edgar's voice murmuring, undoubtedly telling her it was okay, he was in no hurry and Melanie could take all the time she needed.

He'd be a hundred when she'd taken all the time she needed.

"Ready. I'm here. I'm ready." She clumped down the stairs, refusing to descend like a debutante for her assembled company. After all, this was Edgar.

Who looked very nice in charcoal-gray shorts to his knees and a black-and-gray-striped shirt. Very nice. Chic even. Handsome actually. Maybe her heart could calm the hell down now. Because there was Mom glowing at her and glowing at Edgar, her own personal fashion creation, and it was enough to make Melanie want to throw up except she'd barely managed to eat anything today so she probably couldn't even do that.

"Hi, Edgar." She spoke brightly, carelessly. Or...that was how she intended to speak. Unfortunately, it came out like a brittle shriek.

Did this count as a date? Could she go back upstairs now? Because he was looking at her as if she were a combination Virgin Mary and Playboy centerfold, and she wasn't sure she could handle the pressure.

"Hello, Melanie. You look beautiful."

"Oh. Thanks." Smile that felt like a grimace. "You look very nice, too."

"So what's the plan tonight, Edgar?" Tricia was looking nervously at Melanie.

"I thought we'd go to McDonalds for some dinner, then browse around a gaming store for a few hours, maybe end up at DQ for a big ol' Blizzard frozen treat."

Melanie's smile was about to droop in horror when her mother burst out laughing, and Melanie immediately felt ashamed she'd bought it even for a second.

"Boy, Edgar, do you know women or what?" Tricia giggled again.

"I'm pretty sure what." He grinned when she squeezed his forearm affectionately, but he was looking at Melanie, which made Melanie want to look back and also to look away immediately, which she did.

"You'll have a great time." Tricia glanced toward her daughter, made as if to hug her and then changed her mind, making the entire situation even more awkward.

"So. Let's go." Melanie was using that superbright voice again. The sooner they went wherever they were going, the sooner they could be home.

Outside the breeze was cool, the fading sunlight warm. Neighbors had just mowed and the smell of cut grass made her wistful for her childhood in this neighborhood where her most complicated social interaction had been competing with kids on the block for the highest tally of fireflies in a jar.

She got into Edward's car, as perfectly vacuumed and polished and uncluttered as hers was dirty and dusty and full of everything she tossed into it and forgot to take out.

"Where to?"

He gave her that killer smile that did something a little unusual to her insides, and she hoped wherever they went involved plenty of alcohol so she could have some chemical help relaxing. "Fencing."

She was pretty sure they didn't serve alcohol to people with weapons. "Um...really?"

He chuckled and started down the street. "Would you rather do the McDonalds date?"

"No-o-o-o." She wished he wouldn't say *date*. "I've just never been."

"That's why I'm taking you. If you're going to be my girl-friend for all of three dates, you should know about my life outside work."

"Right." She wished he wouldn't say *girlfriend*. "Well, that sounds fun."

It sounded dismal. Fencing? Prancing around with swords? This was what he considered a date? She'd never been on a date anything like that. One guy took her bowling once and that was definitely the end of him.

"No, it doesn't sound fun to you. Not yet. But I think you'll like it."

"I'm sure I will." She didn't mean to, but the words came out sounding as if she'd said, *I'd rather stick pins in my eyes.*

He gave her a sidelong look she couldn't return, which meant he got an eyeful of her staring stoically through the windshield. Poor Edgar. Maybe he'd realize very soon that the idea of the two of them was a really horrible one, and he'd give up tonight and spare them struggling through two more evenings.

They drove several blocks in silence, Melanie unable to help noticing that he drove the car like he was part of it, negotiating turns with grace. She kind of barreled around in Honey the Honda.

Then that idea of him managing a powerful machine with skill started seeming kind of attractive and made her think about him managing her body similarly. She decided it was a great idea to start a conversation.

"What made you start fencing?"

He took so long to answer that she turned to look at him and found he was watching her—luckily they were at a red light—with an odd expression, as if he knew she was trying to make conversation.

"I really want to know, Edgar." Thank God that time her voice came out more naturally.

"Okay." The light changed. The car surged ahead. "I was too small for football, not tall enough for basketball and team sports didn't appeal to me. Maybe it was arrogant, but I liked that fencing match results rested on my own shoulders. I went out there, I won or lost, outcomes were all up to me. The sport suited my loner personality, but also my competitive side."

"I always liked being part of a team."

"Yeah? What did you play?"

"Soccer and softball. Fullback, left field." She sighed, hating that already they were talking like strangers. As though they hadn't been friends for two years. Didn't he see how this dating stuff could ruin everything? "How did you get started in fencing?"

"Dad started me on golf. He got me to play after Stoner refused."

"Why?"

"Rich white country club game. Stoner was all about rebellion."

"Go on."

"So…golf is pretty good discipline, but it wasn't my thing, to Dad's disgust. Anyway, I did meet a guy playing one day who taught fencing at the local rec department, David Shifrin. I took a class and got hooked. He ended up coaching me through high school. We got along really well."

"Better than you and your dad?"

He shot her a surprised look. "Yeah. Dad and I...well, he wanted a carbon copy kid and I wasn't it."

"Neither was Stoner."

"That's for sure."

"Why did you keep at it?"

"Melanie, are you going to ask me questions the entire night?"

"What? What do you mean?"

"You've never been like this with me before."

"I just talked about myself, you mean?"

"That's not what I mean." He merged onto route 41 heading to I94 and downtown. "Is this how you are with men? Once it's a date then you need to flatter me by asking all about me?"

She frowned, thinking. She did ask men questions. It's what you did on dates because men absolutely loved talking about themselves. One of the things she enjoyed about being friends with Edgar was that she could talk about herself, too. Tonight she'd slipped into the old pattern without blinking. "Maybe it's date behavior, yes. But I do want to know. And so I ask."

He laughed. "As long as you really want to know."

"So tell me." She held a pretend microphone in front of her mouth. "Why did you keep at fencing?"

"Because I'm good at it." He grinned at her silly joke. Another thing she enjoyed about Edgar. "Because I love it. Because it keeps me in shape, keeps me social, keeps me improving at something. Life can go around in circles if you don't have a hobby or cause or goal that keeps evolving."

Melanie tried to think of something she kept getting better at. Drinking? Staying out late? Edgar made her feel a little shallow when he made comments like that. She had no idea why he wasn't dating some scholarly type.

Though while he chose one thing and made sure he

improved, she was more about trying out new things. Like when she'd made him pedal out onto Lake Michigan on a Hydrobike.

"Next question?"

She shook her head. "I'm done for now, thank you very much."

He laughed and reached over, rubbed her shoulder, then the back of her neck. His touch was warm and familiar and also not at all. She had to steel herself to keep from flinching from his hands. *Don't touch me.* When he did that, the weird complicated fear started all over, and she'd just been getting comfortable with him again.

She hated having to work to get comfortable with someone she'd already been comfortable with for two years. More comfortable with him than any man she'd ever known. And now he wanted to mess up the best thing she'd ever had, with sex and maybe even love, if she'd heard him right when he left her room the other night. Sex and love never worked out for her. Never.

"Why don't you ask me some questions, Eddie?"

"Is that manly?"

She laughed. "Maybe not traditionally, but women eat it up. If men only knew."

"Okay, then." Another sexy, amused glance. "How are things going with your mom?"

"Oh." Melanie sighed. "She's trying. I'm trying. Though I want to kill her for helping you trick me into bed. What kind of mother does something like that?"

"She wants us to work out."

"Ya think?"

"Would that be so bad?"

"Edgar, don't ask me that."

"Yes, okay, sorry." Another look, a little more serious that time. "She gives great haircuts."

"She always cut Alana's and my hair, too. We loved it.

She'd set up a high stool in front of her vanity, which had a big hinged mirror. We'd pretend we were ladies coming into her shop."

"Not all your memories were bad."

"Definitely not. There's just more of those than the good ones." Melanie shrugged. Ancient history; why dwell on it? "She picked out nice clothes for you, too."

"Nice to have another pair of eyes. Especially ones that can see colors."

It took Melanie a few beats to process that. "You're color-blind?"

"Since birth."

"So that's why…"

"What?" He merged into the left lane to exit onto 94. "I goof up sometimes?"

Most of the time. "Sometimes."

"I thought I had the colors memorized."

"You need someone to help you dress in the morning."

"Want to volunteer?" He grinned at her, and she managed a smile back. Waking every morning with Edgar, to make sure he didn't go to work in green shorts and a brown shirt… The idea appealed to a protective part of her. The rest of her was shouting *no, thanks.*

"You could label your clothes."

He laughed. "I'd look really sharp coming to work with a big tag that said Maroon hanging off my butt."

She giggled. "Better than Kick Me."

"Better than that." He merged efficiently onto the highway, changed lanes and followed the traffic east. "I think your mom is a good person who cares about you and your sister. You can tell by the way she worries."

"Mostly about me." Melanie rolled her eyes.

"She wants you settled."

"So she can stop worrying."

"So you can be happy."

"The way *she* wants me to be happy. The way Alana wants me to be happy. What about the way I want to be happy?"

"How do you want to be happy? Drifting from guy to guy, none of whom gives a shit about you except for the few hours you're wrinkling his sheets?"

"Leave it, Edgar." Deep down she recognized her burst of anger as covering up fear, but she wasn't about to admit that to him. "Since you have a vested interest in this, you're hardly objective on what's best for me."

"Ouch. Yeah, okay, you got me." He signaled and pulled off onto St. Paul Avenue, heading for the Third Ward. "I love you so I'm not allowed to comment."

A bolt of adrenaline zapped her, like lightning. "Don't say that."

"Scary?"

"Yes."

"Well, it's true." He chuckled and pulled into the parking lot of a two-story brick building, parked, turned off the motor and leaned unexpectedly toward her, one hand across the back of her seat, one extended on the dashboard. She felt trapped. He seemed larger than usual, his eyes intense and compelling. He smelled really, really good. "My dream is that one of these days when I'm inside you again and we're making incredible sexual magic happen, I'm going to say it to you and you're going to say it back and mean it."

"Edgar." She was caught, trapped, heart beating in her throat, unable to catch a breath. Where had this version of Edgar come from? "You're kind of freaking me out."

He held her gaze another second; his eyes caught the glow of the rich afternoon sunlight; he seemed unearthly and powerful. Then he blinked, turned and was Edgar again. "Then let's go fence."

He unbuckled his seat belt and got out of the car, leaving her a helpless mess in the front seat. If he was as good with thrust and parry in fencing as he was conversationally, and in bed, it wasn't any wonder he was Wisconsin Division Champion.

The trunk slammed. Her door opened. "You coming?"

She registered him standing with a large long bag, wider at one end, slung over his shoulder, and cleared her gravelly throat. "Yes. Coming."

They walked inside the building and came to a set of doors. To the left were offices. To the right, a reception area and beyond, through another set of doors, these open, a large room with lanes taped off, and fencers in white jackets and masks practicing.

"Hey, Edgar." The cute twenty-something brunette behind the counter beamed at him, dimples showing how glad she was to see him.

"Hi, Carla."

"Scott was hoping you'd be in tonight. Frank got sick and he's looking for a sparring partner."

"I'll see if I can find him. This is Melanie, by the way. Melanie, Carla, who keeps us all in line here. No sneaking past her, no paying late or you're in serious trouble."

Carla giggled. "Nice to meet you, Melanie."

"Same—"

"Hey, Edgar." An athletic-looking middle-aged man waved as he strode by. "Good to see you."

"Hey, Joe." He nudged Melanie. "That's Joe Biebel. World Champion gold medal in 2003, silver in 2008."

"Edgar, my man." Another guy exiting the fencing room paused to give Edgar a high five.

"How's the knee, Ben?"

"Better, thanks." He gave Melanie a nod and moved on.

Melanie felt as if she'd entered an alternate universe where Edgar was the big man on campus, and she the dweeby little nobody. It made her realize to what extent she'd put him in a box and not looked further, and for that she was ashamed.

"Here's the other helmet you asked for. And the jacket. You have everything else you need?"

"Everything. Foils, and my willing prey."

Carla giggled again, then tipped her head to look at him shyly. "A most excellent haircut, Ed-gar."

"Thanks, Carla." He tapped the helmet on the counter in salute, and when he took Melanie's hand to lead her into the club, she let him, feeling oddly passive and uncertain.

"Hey, Edgar. You have time for some practice?" A young blond guy shook Edgar's hand.

"Hi, Scott. I'm here to teach Melanie."

"No, you guys go ahead. I'd like to watch you." The idea of sitting on the sidelines and trying to get a handle on her confusion sounded like heaven. Not to mention putting off the moment where she'd look like an idiot waving around a weapon she had no idea how to use.

"You sure?" Edgar searched her face, and she knew if he thought she was just being polite, he'd turn the guy down.

"Positive." She held his gaze until he seemed satisfied.

"Okay." He found a chair for her, set her up against the wall where she could watch, and explained a few basic rules of combat for foil fencing. The lane they played on was the "piste." Target area was the trunk and groin, front or back. Hits on arms, legs or head didn't count. "Right of way" was in play, which meant the person who attacked first would score the point in the event of a tie.

Sounded simple.

The men suited up, saluted each other by placing the foil straight up in front of their faces, then swishing it down to one side. The helmets reminded her of beekeeper masks; the jackets were covered with padding and thin metal that in competition would register the touches of the sword electronically.

En garde. Allez.

A few minutes later she took back any idea she had about fencing being simple. Since the attacks were varied and lightning fast, the responses had to be instantaneous. Half the time she couldn't even tell what was happening.

Edgar was very...good. She knew nothing about fencing, but even she could tell. Where Scott was bouncing up and down and all over the place, Edgar was solid, calm, steady, graceful, thrusting with power, often relentlessly driving Scott to the very end of the piste, his body holding sharp angles seemingly effortlessly.

He was...sexy. The longer she watched, the more sexy he looked to her, and she started having memories of their nights together and combining those with her view of his body now, controlled and strong and skillful in both cases. She knew the shape of the muscles driving those legs, knew firsthand the strength in those arms.

Oh, my.

A final touch scored and they were done. Edgar pulled off his helmet, his face flushed and damp, grinning with the pleasure of his workout. The pair shook hands, Scott waved to Melanie and left the room.

Edgar came over to her, still grinning, the heat of battle still intense in his gaze now focused on her, and Melanie had to look away.

She wanted him. Right now, out in the parking lot in the car. *Edgar.* Wanted him like crazy, his body, hands and mouth all over her, and hers all over him.

Breathe, Melanie.

She couldn't toy with him. If she was going to make love with him again, it had to be for real. She knew herself, knew she was given to these fickle attractions. She couldn't mess with his mind. Not Edgar. If she hurt him, she'd never forgive herself. He said he was in love with her. She was just horny because he made a very, very hot fencer.

She had to remember who she was and how she dealt with men.

"Ready to learn?"

Melanie laughed to cover her reaction to him. "Sure."

The lesson was agony. He took every opportunity to touch her, and since he'd changed out of the padding that would have put a nice, safe barrier between them, when his body brushed against her, when he guided her legs or arms or torso into position, she got more and more distracted, more and more aware of him sexually and in more and more trouble. Maybe she should run to the ladies' room and bring herself off so she could calm down some.

Except it wouldn't be enough. This wasn't just about orgasms. This was about Edgar, and how he was making her feel. She had to force herself to concentrate on what he was saying, growing so flushed and breathless he probably thought she was in ridiculously bad shape.

Half an hour went by. She'd learned some footwork, some swordwork, and was actually having fun in spite of her sexual torment. The positions were surprisingly difficult but oddly satisfying. It was not unlike dancing, with strict poses and defined movements, yet given what he told her about some simple strategies, also very cerebral.

Melanie wasn't feeling very cerebral. Not at the moment.

Finally, when she was about to beg him for thrusting lessons that had nothing to do with fencing, he glanced at the clock on the wall. "Thanks for indulging me here, Melanie. I hope you enjoyed yourself."

"I did." She smiled at him, thinking she was completely nuts ever to have considered him anything but wildly attractive. "I learned a lot."

"Ready for some dinner?"

"Sure." Oh, no. Dinner. She'd be sitting across the table from him, drinking alcohol, which would lower her resistance. With any luck he'd chosen a nice boisterous hamburger joint where they'd have to shout to be heard and she could lose herself in people watching.

"I made a reservation at Bartalotta's in the village."

Gulp. White tablecloths. Fabulous food. Impeccable service. No guy had ever taken her anywhere that nice. No guy had ever made her feel special enough to be worth it.

Except Edgar.

She was doomed.

10

EDGAR SAT OPPOSITE Melanie at Bartalotta's, wanting to pinch himself. He was having a good time. A really good time. Because he was pretty sure—this was the pinch-himself part—that Melanie was having a really good time, too. No, better than that, a really good *date*. With him.

He'd barely made it through the early part of the evening, wanted to sink through the floor at her lukewarm response to going fencing, but he was determined to show her what he was about so she could decide to take him or leave him.

Too soon to be absolutely sure, but at least she wasn't halfway out the door. In fact, she was sipping her wine happily, making eye contact once in a while, almost shyly, as if—

Okay, he wasn't going that far. But he'd felt the chemistry between them at his club and for once—in daylight, anyway—it wasn't going one way, him lusting after her, her thinking he was dear, sweet, cute Edgar. Tonight…she might have taken the first step toward connecting him in the flesh with the guy she'd responded to so passionately in the dark.

Now he just had to keep it up for two more dates, pray his brother showed her a horrible time, and that Edgar didn't do or say anything to freak her out.

Like "I love you." He'd nearly swallowed his tongue after

those words came out. He hadn't even been planning to say them. At least he'd spoken matter-of-factly, and hadn't dropped to his knees with an earnestly desperate declaration.

She'd be out of the country by now.

He loved spending time with her. He loved the way she got softly looped after he introduced her to a bubbly, crisp Prosecco before dinner. The wine list was excellent, but even given that, everything tasted extra good here. Maybe it was just the atmosphere—elegant but not stuffy. You always had a good time at Bartalotta's.

He loved how she was gradually becoming more talkative as they shared an excellent bottle of Barolo, how she enjoyed her food, ate with relish, didn't pick, or claim diets she wasn't really on.

He loved...her. Tonight was so wonderful. He couldn't get cocky, though, couldn't assume too much. Melanie threw herself headlong into whatever situation she was in while she was in it, and often changed her mind once she got out. She was impetuous, impulsive—everything he wasn't.

"Dessert?"

"Oof." She put her hand to her stomach. "No room."

"Even fruit? Sorbet?"

"I wish." She sighed contentedly, her eyelids drooping sensually.

"Okay." He signaled their waitress for the check and handed over his credit card. "Thanks for joining me tonight."

"Oh, Eddie." Her tone tested his resolve to kiss her sweetly at the door when he dropped her off at home, and leave it at that. "I had a really good time."

"I'm glad." He managed to sound casual, though he wanted to rise from the table and beat his chest. "I had a great time, too."

The waitress came back with his receipt; he signed, then escorted Melanie out into the soft darkness and toward his car.

She yawned and tipped her head up to look at the stars,

staggering slightly. He took her shoulders to steady her. She didn't pull away.

"Mmm, thanks. I had one too many glasses, I guess. I didn't realize until I started trying to walk."

Which meant he would absolutely not try anything. A page out of one of his father's lectures about women, which he swore his mother had put his dad up to when he and Stoner were teenagers. Hard to believe his father would have thought long and hard about how to treat loved ones, considering how he treated his own family. Though, of course, there were people good at spouting theories, and bad at practice.

In any case, ideas of chivalry appealed to Edgar, another reason he enjoyed fencing, where courtesy and sportsmanship were as important as skill. So even though his instinct told him cementing his progress tonight with passion was a good idea, he wouldn't take advantage of Melanie's alcohol-muddled brain.

Darn it.

Her cell phone rang; she fumbled in her purse and peered at the display. He couldn't help seeing it over her shoulder. Stoner.

Confidence started leaking out of him as though he was a tire just gone over a nail. He'd never competed at anything with his brother and won. Stoner wasn't a bad guy, he just needed to come in first, almost pathologically, like their dad. If he got any whiff of Melanie's date tonight with Edgar…

Melanie closed the phone—thank God—and put it back in her purse without answering, which might have killed him. He let go of her soft beautiful shoulders and opened the passenger door for her, hating how the uncertainty that had come so close to vanishing was returning. Would she call Stoner back after he dropped her off at home? Would she go meet him tonight in her tipsy and vulnerable state? Stoner would waste no time taking advantage. Dad's chivalry lectures might as well have been read to the wall in Stoner's case.

Damn it.

Edgar closed the door after she got in, returned her grateful smile, then stalked to the driver's seat. Now what?

He started the engine, telling himself to calm down. They'd had a great time. If she wanted to go screw his brother tonight that was her business. He'd have his answer about her feelings for him, that was for sure. But he didn't relish the idea of staying home alone after a night like this, wondering where they were and what they were doing.

Didn't he just caution himself to calm down? Maybe when Edgar got back home after dropping Melanie off, Stoner would be there happily reading *War and Peace*.

"What's so funny?"

Edgar glanced at her, startled. He must have snorted or something. "Random musings. Nothing worth repeating."

"Okay." She yawned and settled back against the seat.

"I wore you out?"

"No, I'm content. Not that tired."

"Yeah? You want to go get coffee somewhere?"

"Oh, no, Eddie. Thanks. I'll just go home."

Familiar panic rose. He could spend the rest of the night talking to her, this evening had been so miraculous. Obviously she wasn't as fired up as he was.

Okay, okay, one date at a time. This didn't mean she was going to call Stoner, and even if she did, it didn't mean Stoner had won. Edgar had two dates to go.

Still, he drove slowly, savoring the minutes in her presence, sap that he was. At her house, he got out of the car and was prevented from executing a gallant door-opening when she hopped out on her own. They walked to her back door in a silence that became increasingly awkward.

"Well. Thanks, Edgar, for a great evening." She got up on tiptoes to kiss his cheek. "The fencing was great, dinner was delicious, and your company, as always, was—"

He kissed her. Maybe it was a dirty trick in the middle

of her sentence, but she had started looking formal and distant, and a combination of desperation and lust demanded action.

Her mouth was yielding and sweet. Ignoring that her arms rested tautly on his chest instead of wrapping around his neck, he backed her against the door and pushed his thigh between her legs.

"Eddie." Her voice came out a weak gasp when he let her breathe again, and he was satisfied.

Er, no, he wasn't satisfied, he was heated up to the point of taking her against the door, but he was satisfied emotionally with the evening's progress. Satisfied that his kiss had had an effect on her composure.

Which was all he could hope for right now. He'd go home and hope he'd left her wanting more of him. If she went inside and called Stoner, she'd do it with the taste of him still on her lips.

"Good night, Melanie. Thanks for coming out with me."

"Yes. Welcome. Yes." She nodded bemusedly.

"I'll wait until you're safely in."

"Yes. Right. Okay." She fumbled with her keys, dropped them, let him pick them up, and made it into the house.

He grinned and walked a few steps backward, watching her disappear into the kitchen, before he turned to his car and floated the few yards to the driver's side.

Driving home, he couldn't wipe the stupid smile off his face. She'd kissed him back. No, it wasn't daylight, but the back porch light was on, so he hadn't been in darkness this time. She knew he was Edgar and she'd kissed him. With more surrender than passion, but he'd take it.

He pulled into his parking place, bounded up the three flights to his apartment, looking forward to a shower, then some mooning-fantasy time before sleep.

"Dude." Stoner was home. "You were out late."

"Not that late. What is it, eleven?"

Stoner closed the mayonnaise jar, having made his favorite snack, a cheese-and-potato-chip sandwich. "Late for you."

Edgar shrugged. "I had a date."

"Sweet." Stoner put the sandwich on a plate and grabbed a can of beer from the refrigerator, leaving the mayonnaise and dirty knife out, as usual. "Did you get any?"

Edgar sent him a look and poured himself a glass of ice water. "Did you?"

"Nah, I called some friends, but struck out for tonight. I'm going out Friday with your friend Melanie, though. She's going to show me the best clubs in town."

He stopped drinking, his stomach sick. "She called you?"

"I left her a message earlier, then I just called her again, a few minutes before you walked in. She sounded sort of spacy."

"Okay." His stomach settled somewhat. At least she hadn't dialed him the second Edgar left.

"What's her story?"

"What do you mean?" He finished the water, dumped the ice in the sink. He doubted Stoner wanted to know her emotional history.

"She date around or what?"

"She does." He put the glass in the dishwasher, resignedly put the mayonnaise back in the refrigerator.

"Cool. I thought I recognized the type."

"Uh-huh."

"Something bugging you, Edgar?"

"No, why?"

"You get all bent out of shape when the subject is the delectable Ms. Mel-a-nie."

"I guess I'm protective. Big-brother type of friendship and all." He headed for the bathroom so he could stop this hideous lying. "Okay if I sleep in my room tonight?"

"Sure." Stoner put his feet up on the coffee table and turned on the TV. "I think you got it bad for her."

Edgar stopped a foot from his bedroom door, already taking off his shirt. "Me?"

"That whole big-brotherly thing?" Stoner shook his head, mouth full of cheese, bread and potato chips. "Not buying it."

"Okay." He pulled his shirt back down, took a few steps back into the living room until he was in Stoner's field of vision, arms crossed over his chest. "If I said yeah, I'm in love with her, would it make a difference to you Friday night?"

Stoner laughed. "Dude, if the woman wants me, she wants me." He swallowed a bite. "Are you in love with her?"

"Yeah."

Stoner put his sandwich down. "How about that."

"Yeah. How about that."

"She love you?"

Edgar shrugged.

"You were out with her tonight?"

"Yeah."

"Progress?"

"Maybe."

Stoner nodded thoughtfully. "Well, shit. That does change things."

"Yeah?"

"Yeah. Now I'll just have her give me a blow job."

"Geez, Stoner, I—"

"I'm *kidding*. Lighten up. Man, you *do* have it bad."

Edgar unclenched his fist, forced himself to start breathing again. "Sorry."

"Let me tell you something." He picked up his can of Budweiser. "You want to stay intact? Keep your heart and your dick separate. Love will tear you apart, man."

Too late. Way too late. "Uh…"

Stoner sighed. "You're whipped. I can tell."

"Couldn't help it."

"Yeah, I know. Believe it or not, I got hit once, too."

"You?" Edgar dropped onto the couch next to his brother.

"Remember Jessica Barnes?"

"You dated senior year."

"I was nuts about her. Nuts. She said jump, I asked how far. Pathetic." He took a long swig of beer. "I did this for two years, then she dumped me. I was like that's it, my life is over. Over, man. I didn't think I could ever feel happy again."

"I remember."

"That's when I said okay, that's it for me. No more of this. I never, ever want to feel that way again, never want to be so vulnerable to someone that she can make me feel that kind of pain again. Never. And I know it's against what you're supposed to be like, but I'm happy. I'm just really effing happy now without all that angst."

For a brief moment, Edgar understood him; he might even have agreed with him. Possibly a first in their relationship. But then he remembered what Melanie's mouth felt like pressed against his, and he knew his brother was wrong in every way it was possible to be wrong.

A commercial for a floor cleaner came on TV. They both sat watching, though Edgar was pretty sure neither of them was paying attention.

"I'll keep my hands to myself. You don't need me making trouble. You've got plenty already."

Edgar nodded, his throat actually tightening with emotion. He'd underestimated his brother. "Thanks, Ben."

"That's Mr. Stoner to you."

"Right."

"So, uh, I stopped by your coffee shop this morning. That Kaitlin you told me about? She's something, huh?" He pulled his feet abruptly off the coffee table. "She heard us play last year and came again to Waukesha. She had all these ideas about how we can market ourselves bigger, all these fantastic ideas for our Web site and stuff. She thinks we're good."

"You are good."

"Yeah, so I invited her to come hear us play Bad Genie Rock Lounge tomorrow." He cleared his throat, drank some more beer. Belched. Put his feet back up on the table. Took them down again.

Edgar started grinning; he punched his brother lightly on the arm. "Kaitlin's great. A great girl. Kind of looks like *Jessica,* too, don't you think?"

"Shut up." He glowered at Edgar. "She couldn't stop talking about *you.* At least at first."

"Yeah?" Edgar held out his hands, what-can-I-do? "You know, I just rake them in. Can't help it. It's my animal magnetism."

"Yeah, squirrel or something." He whapped Edgar on the shoulder. "Chipmunk, maybe."

Edgar chuckled and got up to take his shower. Date number two with Melanie to look forward to. Stoner out of the picture. Right now he felt like a freaking lion. "Good luck with Kaitlin. And thanks for keeping it zipped Friday."

"You already thanked me. Don't start getting all girlie on me or I'll do Melanie up against the wall and make you watch."

"Ha." He wished he could say no way would Melanie go for that, but maybe she would. He wouldn't. He wanted her all to himself.

And he was starting to allow himself the luxury of hoping that someday soon he'd have exactly that.

11

MELANIE STOOD IN THE middle of the kitchen, listening to Edgar's car drive away. She didn't feel the way she usually felt after first dates. Usually she was keyed up and blissful. All night—or all morning—she would replay key moments and giggle, hugging the memories to her.

Tonight she felt somber and uneasy, close to tears. Images of Edgar seemed to be competing in her brain. The sweet geek who was her best friend. The sex god in the darkness. The powerful fencer wielding his sword skillfully and unmercifully.

Freud would have a field day with that last one.

She poured herself a glass of water, drank it down, refilled it and emptied that one, too. She needed to talk to someone; she needed company. Jenny was out tonight with Noah. Alana would be in bed already, asleep or not asleep with Sawyer; she wouldn't want to have an extended girl talk at this hour. Of course she didn't really enjoy extended girl talks at any hour, though she was getting better since Sawyer. Ironically, usually when Melanie was upset she talked it out with Edgar. In this case, obviously, she couldn't.

Her cell rang; she fumbled for it eagerly. Maybe it was Jenny. Alana. Edgar...

It was Stoner. Again. What did he want that he'd call her twice in one evening?

"Hi, Stoner."

"Hey, Mel-a-nie."

She waited for the thrill of his deep voice singing her name. It came, but only halfheartedly. "What's up? Sorry I couldn't call back sooner."

"Out on a date?"

"Uh. Yes." She screwed her eyes shut, praying he wouldn't ask anything else.

"I was sitting around tonight with nothing to do. I started thinking we should, you know, get together and everything."

"Oh." Sitting around with nothing to do. The date was about his boredom, not about her. That she understood. That she'd encountered time and time again with guys she'd dated. She closed her eyes, remembering Edgar, that second night in bed when she'd been trying so hard to push him away. *Because, Melanie. It's always been about you for me.*

"What's up with you Friday? My band isn't doing anything. You can show me the city nightlife. What do you say?"

What the hell was she supposed to do now?

The answer came immediately. *Go.* The deal with Edgar was three dates with him, as many as she wanted with his brother. She knew exactly what to expect out of a date with Stoner, and could handle every aspect of it. City nightlife with hot rock 'n' roll dudes. Like a performance of a show she'd been in a thousand times. Nothing would surprise her, nothing would unbalance her.

Nothing would touch her.

"Sounds great, Stoner."

"Excellent. Pick me up at nine?"

She pictured herself showing up at his apartment where he and Edgar sat in the living room, and selecting Stoner for that evening's entertainment.

God, no. "Can you wait outside so, um, I don't have to find a place to park?"

"Sure thing, babe. Friday at nine. I'll be there."

"See you then." She clicked off the phone.

Okay then. A date with Stoner. Just him and her experiencing the wild side.

Ho-hum.

She grimaced, set the glass by the side of the sink and trudged upstairs, lonely, empty, wistful for something she couldn't grasp.

This wasn't how she was supposed to feel with a date with Edgar behind her and one with Stoner to look forward to. For one thing, the date with Edgar was supposed to make everything crystal clear. He was a friend or he was her lover. Instead, he was sort of both. And sort of neither.

A glimmer of light shone from under her mom's bedroom door. Mom and Alana, the great sleep-deprived duo, though Alana was apparently sleeping better since Sawyer. Since Sawyer—SS. Like BC or AD, a.m. or p.m. An enormous change, before and after.

Melanie hesitated in the hallway. Did she want to talk to Mom? She might be the best person, since she had plenty of, uh, experience with men. Maybe she'd felt like this about someone. Maybe she'd figured it out and could share her insight.

At the same time, after practically shoving Melanie into bed with Edgar, she wasn't going to be an impartial listener.

However, at this hour, she was the only listener available.

Melanie knocked softly, thinking how remarkable it was to be coming to her mother with a problem. She'd probably gone before with scraped knees and broken toys, but this was a first. An important first, one she couldn't have foreseen even a couple of weeks ago.

A pause, then a soft, "Come in, Melanie."

Tricia was sitting in a cross-legged meditation position. Her eyes were open, but her face and body were absolutely still and calm. Peaceful. What a concept.

"You need to teach me that, Mom."

Tricia patted the floor next to her. "No time like the here and now. How was your date?"

"Oh, it was …" She gestured aimlessly. "It was…"

To her horror, her voice shook. A tear fought for the right to spill down her cheek, and won.

Tricia grinned in delight. "Threw you for a loop, huh?"

"Is that what this is?" She plunked down beside her mom, surprised to feel comfortable in the mother-daughter moment. "Does meditation cure loops?"

"It cures everything. Come on. Sit comfortably. Rest your hands on your knees, palms up. If you want you can touch your thumb and index finger together."

"Okay." Melanie crossed her legs, arranged her hands, pictured herself chanting "ommm" and had to stifle a giggle. "I'm ready."

"First, relax. Start at your toes, go through every body part, finish at the top of your head. Then let your mind go blank."

"That's it?"

"That's it."

"How do I know I'm doing it right?"

"Because you can't do it wrong. If you want, set yourself thinking about Edgar. Sometimes you can hear an internal voice giving you true answers."

"Oh, man, I'd love some truth." She settled herself, relaxed her muscles toes to crown, and tried like hell to clear her mind. That part didn't work so well. She tried some more. Her knee started to ache. Her nose itched.

"Stop wiggling, Melanie. Just be."

"I'm trying." She tried again. And then again. And found

herself getting frustrated. But the vision of her mother's clear, calm face kept her going.

How do I feel about Edgar?

Nothing.

How do I feel about Edgar?

Nothing. Her mind started wandering.

Edgar...the look on his face when he'd trapped her in the car. *My dream is that one of these days when I'm inside you again and we're making incredible sexual magic happen...*

Sparks and heat burned through her system.

Great. Instead of peace and oneness with the universe, she was just getting horny.

A chirping filled the room. Melanie opened her eyes in confusion. Tricia made a sound of exasperation.

"My phone, sorry. I forgot to turn it off." She grabbed her cell from her purse lying by her bed, checked the display. Her eyes lit up. "Mind if I take this?"

"No, of course not." Anything to get out of meditating.

"Hi." Tricia's voice was soft, intimate. She got up from the floor and started pacing. "What's going on? No, you're not calling too late. I was just teaching Melanie how to meditate on her issues."

A man. Mom was talking to a man, maybe the same one as before. Melanie had to quell the instinctive anger. This was fine. Mom was a big girl. She was clean. She was sober. The guy could be a friend, though from the way her mom had brightened, Melanie doubted it.

"Yes, tomorrow. Okay, I'll be there. Thanks so much, Jim." She snapped the phone off. "Now where were we?"

"Oh, no." Melanie folded her arms across her chest. "You don't get off that easy. Who was that?"

"An old friend."

"Old boyfriend?"

"No." She pressed her lips together, started to speak, then

stopped. Melanie waited. "He was a friend of your father's and mine."

Melanie stared. Tricia had never told them about their father other than that they'd dated for a while and he'd left. "Is he...like Dad?"

"Not really. Well, we were all stupid in those days. He's been clean longer than I have. Ten times longer. And he was always more stable than your dad. More emotionally honest. More in touch with his feelings." She rolled her eyes. "Naturally, that's why I didn't fall for him."

Melanie nodded sympathetically. "I hear you."

"Anyway, it's nice to be back in touch."

Back in touch? That could mean anything. She was still leery of any guy Mom invited into her life, old friend or not, which was silly. "Is this a date?"

"No, no, no. No. This is not a date. No."

Right. "Mom?"

"Yes?" She smoothed her skirt nervously, her voice as chirpy as her cell phone.

"Maybe you could say *no* a few more times?"

"Oh." She laughed uneasily. "He's taking me to meet a friend of his who writes children's books, to show her my drawings."

"Really?" No, that wasn't a date. Maybe Jim was okay if he was helping her mother pursue this new, cool career. It sounded like something Edgar would do. "That is very sweet of him."

"It is, isn't it." Her mother's cheeks grew pink. "Why don't we get back to meditating?"

Melanie grinned slyly to let her know her change of subject wasn't unnoticed. Sounded as if this man *was* more than an old friend to her mother. Maybe Mom's taste in men had improved along with her habits and attitude.

Was that all it took? Melanie settled herself back down on the floor, determined this time to do better at meditation.

And, actually, after she relaxed, she did manage to push most of her thoughts away. In fact, she was really starting to—

Her mother fidgeted beside her.

Melanie returned to her own mind, cleared it again. Tried to make sure that—

Tricia scratched.

Melanie opened her eyes. "Stop wiggling, Mom. Just *be*."

Tricia looked startled, then burst out laughing. "Okay. How about we just talk?"

"Much better. It's too late for concentrating. I'll practice again tomorrow." She got up and sat on the bed, pleased when her mother joined her.

"So tell me about the date with Edgar. What did you do?" She blinked innocently. "How was the DQ Blizzard?"

Melanie scowled at her. "We went fencing."

"Fencing! Now that is an unusual date. I had a guy take me cow-tipping once, but that is cooler. I assume he knows what he's doing?"

"He's Wisconsin Division Champion. Cow-tipping?"

"Long time ago. Go on with Edgar, I'm impressed."

"He was...different there." Melanie flopped back on the bed. "Everyone knew him and liked him and respected him. I saw him spar with a friend and he was really good, confident and graceful, really in his element."

"How did that make you feel?" She snorted in that way that reminded Melanie of Alana. "Apparently I'm your therapist for the evening."

Melanie managed a smile. "Disconcerted."

"Like he was breaking out of the safe little box you had him in? And how dare he?"

Astonished, she turned to stare at her mother. "Yes, that's it. Damn, you are good."

Tricia rolled her eyes. "If it's an emotion you can have for a man I've not only had it, but analyzed it in deep detail with a professional. I could write a book."

"Maybe you should."

"Go on." She pretended to hold a pad and pen to take notes. "What did you do after the fencing?"

Melanie giggled, wistful for all the years she'd missed with Tricia. "Dinner. At Bartalotta's in the village."

Tricia whistled silently. "The man knows his food."

"Mmm." Melanie sighed rapturously. "It was wonderful food."

"And the rest? How did it feel? Your therapist wants to know."

"We drank Prosecco and talked and it was easy and nice the way it always is with Edgar. Except..."

"Except?"

She grimaced. "I had, um, feelings that weren't easy and nice the way it always is with Edgar."

"Lu-u-st." Tricia drew out the word, relishing her pronouncement. "I'm not surprised. He does have a *great* haircut."

"He does." She shared another laugh with her mother and felt some of her disturbance subsiding.

"What's next?"

"I promised to go on three dates with him. Then I have to decide whether I still consider Edgar in...*that* way."

Would she? Wouldn't she? All she knew was that she was in this mess deeper than she ever would have anticipated.

"Then Stoner called and now I have a date with him, too."

"Good."

"Good?" The last reaction she expected.

"Comparison shopping."

Melanie giggled again, put her hands under her head. "I think this might drive me completely insane."

"Why do you think that's so?"

"Because he was a friend for so long, and then he was a lover without me knowing it. What is he now? And what if this ends up screwing up our friendship? I don't know what I'd do without him." She got up on her elbows, focused on Mr. August from her firefighter calendar. "He's always there for me, he listens when I'm upset, he tolerates my insanity, he accepts every flaw I have. I've never met anyone like that before. If I lose him because of this..."

Tricia shrugged. "Don't lose him. He's certainly not going anywhere if the vibe I get from him is true. The guy is completely in love with you."

Adrenaline again. Why wouldn't it behave itself? "I just can't...date him. I can't be in a romance with Edgar."

"Who says you have to be in a romance? Go on the next two dates. See how you feel then." Tricia patted Melanie's knee. "You don't have to decide anything tonight."

"You're right. It's just that...I...he..." She gave up, collapsed back onto the bed. Here's where things got really fuzzy. She had no rational responses, just feelings. "I'm terrified."

"Of what?" Her mother lay down next to her, stared up at the ceiling alongside her.

"I don't even know."

"I do."

"What? Commitment?"

"No, not commitment." Her mother shook her head, making a swishy sound against the rose-colored quilt. "You're scared because you're falling in love."

12

TRICIA WAITED IMPATIENTLY on the stairs for Jim to arrive. Since their last lunch meeting, she'd meditated over him several times, and though her inner voice had been silent, she'd decided it was in everyone's best interest that they stay friends. First and foremost, because she'd promised herself no men in Milwaukee. Her duty here was to her daughters, and they did not need to see her getting messed up in a romance. She wanted to prove to them she'd moved beyond her man-dependence, and the worst way to do that was to fall in with someone less than a month after she'd returned. Second, she was moving to Florida, so what was the point of starting something with Jim that was doomed to end in a few months? And third, she needed this time without men for herself, too. Since adolescence she'd been attached to some male or other with mere weeks in between. This was her time, finally, to bloom on her own, to find out who she was and what she could accomplish.

Better late than never.

All morning she'd been making the rounds, applying for jobs at restaurants and hair salons. The process had been exhausting and oddly discouraging. Yes, she needed income, but something about pursuing the same old employment felt like taking a step backward for the first time since she'd started her recovery a year ago.

She was irritable now, and craving a cigarette. On this trip she'd have to have the dreaded "talk" with him, to tell him her decision, which made her even more jittery and cranky. Then she'd have to meet a woman who'd pass some kind of official judgment on her work. She wished Jim would show up soon so she could at least get that part over with.

A motorcycle engine sounded, growing louder. Had he brought the bike? She leaned out to look down the street, and Jim came into view riding the old Harley, looking every bit the hot biker rebel he'd been a quarter century before. Her jitters increased, but her crankiness fell victim to a genuine welcoming smile. No matter what, an old friend was a sight for lonely eyes.

"Hi there." He turned off the bike, grinning as if his eyes had been lonely, too, took off his helmet and climbed off, headed for her—a man on a mission.

She turned her face so his mouth regretfully landed on her cheek. "Hi, Jim. Thought you'd bring the car today."

"Thought about it." He looked at her curiously. "But the bike could use a real ride, and I thought maybe you'd like that, too."

"Yes. Yes." She managed a tight smile over a seriously shaken resolve. The way he strode possessively toward her in his black leather jacket and jeans... Oh, boy. "Um, can we talk for a second before we go?"

She'd counted on having this conversation in the car, not in the driveway, but she wasn't going to shout at him en route on the bike. Not for a topic like this.

"Sure." He folded his arms across his broad chest. "What's on your mind, Tee?"

"Us, I guess. You and me. What this is all about." She gestured between them, all hope of being able to gracefully lead into the subject gone. "I mean, last time in the van, it wasn't—I don't think…"

"Too much too soon?"

Tricia blew out a breath, more anxious about hurting or disappointing him than getting what she knew was right for her. Typical, putting consideration of men's feelings ahead of hers. But she wouldn't back down. She was learning. "Yes. Exactly. Too fast. It was a surprise. Seeing you, and all those memories. But…I'm not looking to get involved with anyone right now."

"I had a feeling." He looked at her seriously, but didn't seem upset. "It's why I didn't throw you over my shoulder and haul you upstairs to your bedroom just now. The only reason."

She felt herself blushing fiercely. Holy moly.

"Thanks, Jim. That would have been…" *Delicious. Sexy. Incredible.* "Inappropriate."

"Inappropriate." He rolled his eyes. "Who are you and what have you done with the real Tricia Hawthorne?"

She laughed again, gratefully warm and fuzzy. He'd made this easy for her, accepting her needs without question, while flattering her by making sure she understood he wasn't accepting them because he wanted to. "Thanks for understanding."

"I do. I don't like it, I admit, but I understand. You're in a different place right now than I am. If you'd shown up ten years ago and pushed for involvement when I was first getting my life back on track, I would have done the same…." He frowned, scratched his forehead. "Nah, I'd still have jumped you."

Tricia burst out laughing, leaned forward and gave him a spontaneous hug and kiss…on the cheek, sigh. "You're the best, Jim."

"You are so right." He grinned and smacked her lower back—low enough that she gave him a warning glare that didn't bother him in the slightest. "Let's go. Beatrice is dying to meet you."

"I'm ready."

Tricia followed him onto the motorcycle, settled herself, and spent the next two hours relaxed and happy. Almost relaxed. Relaxed would have been possible only if she could have kept herself from thinking about the broad strong back in front of her and how fun it would be to lean into it, tease him with the feel of her breasts, maybe slide her hands around to the front, tease him more, touch him when no cars were nearby, drive him insane so he'd pull off the road and—

Incorrigible. She was incorrigible.

And relaxed would have been more possible if she didn't feel as if driving two hours to find out what this woman thought of her pictures was overkill. She liked them or she didn't. All this emphasis on a face-to-face meeting made Tricia nervous.

Milwaukee turned to farmland within half an hour's drive; farmland alternated with forest to Madison. Beyond Madison to the north, the landscape began to swell and fall with gentle treed hills. Off Route 188, they followed back roads through more farmland until they climbed to the top of a particularly high and beautiful rise and turned into a driveway leading to a lovely stone farmhouse shaded by maples and edged with daylilies in more colors than Tricia knew existed.

"Here we are." Jim secured the bike after Tricia climbed off. "Beatrice's place. She's lived here about eight years now."

Tricia pulled off her helmet and inhaled the sweet fresh air sweeping across the hills, trying not to feel she was about to go on trial. She hadn't been to this part of the state since she was a kid and her parents brought her on a minivacation for a tour of the Wollersheim Winery on their way to Wisconsin Dells. It wasn't Colorado or the Pacific Northwest, but it had a good deal more charm than the unrelenting flatness of the southeastern part of the state.

"Nice, isn't it?"

"Beautiful house. And what a view." She swept her helmet toward the valley below, then surrendered it to Jim.

"Welcome."

Tricia turned, taken aback when the grandmotherly figure she'd been picturing for whatever reason turned out to be a woman younger than she was. Er, not *much* younger. She was stunning, with long wavy auburn hair, fresh natural skin and lively eyes, dressed in a floral skirt and cream top that hugged her slender figure. By the adoring look she gave Jim and the way he gathered her in for a bear hug, Tricia decided she'd have to hate her.

Except when she turned to Tricia her eyes were warm. "Hi, Tricia, I'm so glad to meet you. Come in, I have homemade strawberry lemonade and cookies waiting."

"Thank you, it's nice to meet you, too." She guessed. "Your house is beautiful. Did you plant the flowers yourself?"

"The previous owners did those. I planted the kitchen garden on the other side of the house, though." Her smile was gracious, relaxed. She moved so like a dancer she made Tricia feel like an elephant with a broken leg. "Not that we can grow all that much in our short summer here."

"No." She thought of Dahlia, eating out of her garden in California practically all year long. "Jim said you'd lived here eight years?"

"I moved a few years after my divorce. I needed a change. I left a lot of bad things behind in the city. But I'm also a loner and I really do prefer the peace. This feels like home by now."

"How are the winters?" Tricia would go insane within three weeks of a snowfall.

"Long. But I also have a house in Florida."

"Florida." Tricia half laughed in surprise. "Where?"

"Kissimmee. Not far from Orlando." She stopped to pick an invasive morning glory vine out of a bed of impatiens. "We'll have to get together after you move. Jim visits often. He's been checking out real estate, too."

Tricia sent him a quizzical glance. Jim in Florida? She couldn't quite imagine that. "Really?"

Jim shrugged. "It's a dream still. No serious plan."

"Come on in." Beatrice opened the door and stepped aside for them to precede her. "We're set up on the patio."

The house was as beautiful inside as out, with casual welcoming furniture, lots of thriving plants. The patio had a different view of the valley and of an expansive vegetable garden bordered by roses in bloom. What a life! As peaceful, clean, spacious and solitary as Tricia's past decades had been stressful, dirty, cramped and crowded.

They sat on comfortable cushioned iron chairs. The strawberry lemonade was fruity and not too sweet, the spiced butter cookies made Tricia vow to improve her baking. A breeze swept through the screens, butterflies and bees visited the garden, and Tricia thought she even saw a hawk soaring over the hill. Heavenly.

They chatted a little, Jim and Beatrice catching up on a few people Tricia didn't know, then on his studio work and Beatrice's publishing career, which appeared to be going very well; she was selling steadily. Tricia imagined what that would be like, not having to go anywhere to work, living in your creative head all day long. That might work for her....

But what about her pictures?

"Tricia." Beatrice turned toward her as if she'd heard her thoughts. "I have to admit that when Jim said he wanted to show me a friend's drawings I only said yes because I love him."

"Oh." Tricia wasn't sure what she was supposed to say to that.

"As you should," Jim said.

"Don't take offense. You wouldn't believe how often authors are asked to look at other people's work. I stopped saying yes because the truth is, it doesn't matter what I think. Your work needs to impress an agent or an editor and eventually your readers. *They're* the ones who can get you someplace, not me. I'm just one opinion and mine doesn't matter."

"Okay." She tried to hide her disappointment, not even aware until that minute how much she'd wanted the validation of a professional opinion. Why would Beatrice want them to come up here just so she could say she couldn't help?

"However." She reached down to get a folder beside her chair. "I have to say this little calendar witch absolutely stole my heart. She's wonderful. I'd go out on a limb and say you have something big here."

"Thank you so much." Tricia spoke breathlessly. A delicious feeling of pride started choking out her nerves. She glanced at Jim, who was grinning as if she'd just won a Pulitzer.

Beatrice opened the folder, paged through the sheets, laughing occasionally. "I love this idea of stealing time. Not only that, stealing holidays—good times with family and friends, time away from work and duties. I think that's something everyone can relate to. We all have calendar witches in our lives."

Tricia nodded, trying to get past the pleasure-buzz to listen to what Beatrice was saying. She hadn't thought through why the adventure appealed to her so much, but yes, of course, there it was. The crime of someone stealing away your special time with family. Two children fighting to get it back. How obvious.

"I illustrate my own stories, so I can't work with this one. I do have a friend in Texas looking for an illustrator, but if you really want to know..." She closed the folder. "I wanted to meet you before I suggested this, to get a feel for who you are, or as much as anyone can in half an hour, but honestly,

I think you should write your own story. In many ways you already have with these pictures. It's just a question of finding the words that go with them."

Huh? Tricia gaped at her. "Oh, gosh, I'm not a writer."

"Maybe not. But it's worth a try. I'm happy to help if you want."

"You said you hate helping other people." She spoke impulsively, then wanted to smack herself.

Beatrice seemed unfazed. She smiled at Jim. "Let's say in this case I'm willing to make an exception."

Tricia froze. She did not want to hear any more about this.

Jim cleared his throat. "I photographed her daughter's wedding last year. She seems to think she owes me favors."

"He forgot to mention he wouldn't let me pay him." She put her hand on Jim's arm. "Don't let this man go, Tricia. You'll regret it forever. Trust me."

Tricia laughed to cover her embarrassment. Beatrice obviously thought they were involved; it seemed rude to contradict her. "We lost touch for a lot of years. I won't make that mistake again."

"Good."

"I don't want to impose on your time if you don't like—"

"Let her help, Tricia. You can learn from her." His gray eyes were watching her steadily. "She wouldn't offer if she didn't want to."

"He's right. I genuinely love the drawings and think you have a great and highly marketable story. I'd enjoy helping you." She patted Jim's arm. "We'll just not mention that Jim threatened to bomb my house if I said no."

Tricia's head whipped around to Jim; he was laughing.

"Now that—" he picked up his lemonade and toasted her "—was a sick joke, dear."

"Wasn't it?" Beatrice smiled warmly at Jim again, and Tricia's intuition told her there had been something between these two once upon a time. She couldn't blame Jim. There was a graceful, sexual quality that lightened and complimented Beatrice's solid, earth mother warmth.

The three of them chatted, about Florida, Wisconsin, California. Stories came out—Jim apparently met Beatrice at one of his initial AA meetings and they hit it off right away. Beatrice demanded stories of Jim and Tricia's misspent youth.

At a natural lull in the conversation, Jim thanked Beatrice for the lemonade and cookies and Tricia thanked her for the lovely comments about her book and promised to try her hand at writing the story, a promise she wasn't at all sure she had the courage or chops to keep.

On the way down the driveway Tricia waved and looked back more than once to see the lovely hilltop house receding behind them. She didn't know why the idea of Beatrice living there by herself made her feel wistful and a bit sad. Maybe it was that living in the middle of nowhere like that would make Tricia stark raving bonkers.

Half an hour later, Jim pulled into the parking lot of a takeout barbecue restaurant just as Tricia was about to yell that she needed a bathroom. While she went, he loaded up on food, then drove them to Devil's Lake State Park for a picnic.

The lake was a gorgeous blue surrounded by forested, rocky hills. Fluffy white clouds floated overhead and an eagle soared over the water looking for his dinner.

They set their food on a picnic table and dug into the juicy, fragrant meat, white rolls and coleslaw, hardly talking while they ate, relishing the view and the delicious meal, the quiet companionship more valuable just then than anything they could say.

"I miss beer the most with food like this." Jim set down a rib and picked up another.

"Same here. It's worth it, though, to know we'll get home alive."

He chuckled. "Pretty good incentive, huh?"

"The best." She pushed her plate away. One more bite and she'd explode. "Thank you for taking me to see Beatrice, Jim. I wasn't sure what to expect but I liked her a lot."

"She's something. Designs her own jewelry, paints, raises chickens, has a huge garden, fruit trees. She is as self-sufficient as possible."

"I'm trying to be the same. Without the chickens." Tricia licked her fingers. "How long did you date her?"

"Can't get anything by you." He grinned and touched her hand. "For about a year. We joined AA at the same meeting. She was going through a divorce, I'd just broken up with someone...we both needed a body to lean on. But we weren't right for each other. I couldn't live out there in the boonies and she hated the city."

"She's lovely."

"You noticed that, huh?"

Tricia kicked him under the table.

He laughed. "What did you think about her suggestion you write your own book?"

"It's totally beyond me."

"Geez." He rolled his eyes. "There's my Tricia, brimming with can-do arrogance."

She snorted and kicked him again. "I'm serious. I'm not a writer. I barely got through high school."

"So reenroll. Take some classes. Find out if you have any talent."

She collected her plate, napkins and plastic to give herself time to process what he'd just said. Classes. "I never thought of that."

"Because you haven't started looking ahead yet. You will, though. Right now you're so glad to be out of the crap that it feels fabulous just being alive and awake some days, and on others you're still fighting the pull of various chemicals. That's enough to deal with right now. But it won't be forever.

Soon the urges will be manageable, and not spiraling down isn't going to be enough. You'll want to move forward. When that hits, you'll know. And you have a goal already."

Her throat swelled uncomfortably. What was it about this man that moved her so deeply? "Your goal was pictures."

"Mine was building my studio, yes. It's gone well." He wiped his hands clean with a napkin, added it to their trash bag and turned to look out at the lake. "Now I have other goals."

"What are those?"

"Ah, Tricia." He didn't continue, sat looking out at the water, a slight frown wrinkling his brow.

She felt an unreasonable fear, without any clue as to its source. "Jim?"

"Hmm?"

"Are you okay?" She leaned forward and touched his arm. "You left me there."

"Sorry, I got distracted. My goal right now   " he leaned down to dig through his bag and came up with a camera "—is to take your picture."

"Oh, God, no." She waved him away. "I hate having my picture taken."

"Tough. Stand up. Come over by the lake."

Tricia rolled her eyes. "Do I have to, Dad?"

"Yup." He held out his hand. She took it in exasperation and let him haul her to her feet, hold it while she extracted herself from the picnic table.

He found a place he thought would suit for her portrait after four or five tries that involved climbing over rocks toward a huge cliff, while she got more and more cranky, and he got more and more cheerful and enthusiastic.

"This is it. Perfect."

"Here?"

"Up. We'll climb there."

"Up where, there?" She pointed to a nearby flat ledge.

"Nope." He pointed higher. "There."

"What?"

"I'll be right behind you."

"Do I look like a mountain goat?"

He gave her a severe look and jabbed his finger toward the spot. "Climb."

She crossed her arms over her chest, feeling a silly hot thrill at her rebellion. "And if I refuse?"

He held her gaze, leaned forward. "I'll kiss you until you can't breathe anymore."

Her swallow was audible over the lapping of the lake.

"Okay." She had to clear her throat. "Okay, I'm climbing."

"Good girl."

Tricia sputtered in disgust. "Girl? I'm sorry, am I your puppy?"

"Ungh. Good wo-man." He put caveman emphasis on the phrase, which cracked her up.

The climb wasn't as bad as it looked from the bottom, and in about five minutes she'd reached the ledge he'd spotted, and arranged herself. The cliff rose up about five hundred feet beyond them, but he better think this was far enough or she'd push him off into the lake.

"That's it. The late afternoon sun is perfect. You'll glow."

"From sweat?"

"Your inner light." He looked through the lens, focused, stepped around a bit checking the angle, the background, moved her three more times until she was getting ready for that oh-so-satisfying shove.

"Now smile. Be happy."

She tried. She really tried. But every time she thought she had a lovely happy smile going, he'd make a sound of impatient disapproval.

"What?"

"Don't try so hard. Be yourself." He shifted his footing. "Look out into the lake. Just enjoy it. Forget the smiling."

She stopped smiling. Looked. Tried to be herself. "Should I meditate?"

"If that helps relax you, sure."

Tricia nodded, lengthened her spine, drew in some breaths, closed her eyes for a count of five then opened them again, relaxed her body, let her mind go free.

"There. The-e-ere." He drew the word out the way someone does when you're giving him a massage and you hit just the right spot. She wondered if she'd be able to resist him if he ever came on to her in spite of her request that he not.

And in the next thought she realized that Jim never would. And that he was probably the finest man she'd ever known. Accepting her, encouraging her to reach beyond what had become her limited but safe new life. Quietly making opportunities for her to keep moving forward, to keep her from slipping back.

Good man. She was so lucky he'd come back into her life.

No, she didn't believe that. No such thing as luck. No such thing as accidents. He'd come back into her life because he was fated to. Because she needed him. And maybe he needed her, too.

The camera clicked, clicked again, startling her; she laughed, having practically forgotten he was there. *Click. Click.*

"Look back into the lake. Keep thinking about whatever you were thinking about."

"Okay." She looked back into the lake. Kept thinking about Jim, though her thoughts gradually became less noble, and strayed in spite of her best efforts, to include his kisses, his strength, his passionate intensity. *Click, click, click click click click.*

"God, you're beautiful."

She turned, startled again, and found him watching her over the camera. She wasn't beautiful. She was gray and prematurely aged by the violence she'd done her body, chemically speaking, and she could lose ten pounds and not miss them.

But with Jim she felt beautiful, young, healthy...sane, even.

He sat beside her and they watched the sun gradually lower, the light grow richer and more golden, the colors of the lake and the woods deepen. Tricia felt more content, more complete than she could remember ever feeling in her life. The joyful peace she usually had to meditate to experience had come automatically, just being here with Jim.

And it hit her that when she moved to Florida and left him here, she'd fall to pieces and have to build up a new life all over again, this time without him.

13

MELANIE PULLED UP in front of Edgar's apartment building and checked her messages. Still nothing from Stoner about this date they were supposed to have had the previous night, which he'd canceled and promised to reschedule. Typically unreliable. Hard to imagine she'd spent so much time nuts over annoying self-centered men like that.

At this point she was ready to say forget it and good riddance, which wasn't like her. Usually she loved beating her head against the brick wall of unrequited longing. Maybe this change was a good thing. Progress toward self-esteem. If nothing else, maybe Edgar would raise the bar for her future relationships.

Tonight, their second date, he was cooking a fancy dinner for her at his apartment, another first. Previous dates all shared her taste for crowds and loud music, late nights and plenty of alcohol. If any of them could cook gourmet food, they hadn't bothered showing off that talent for her.

Melanie looked her car, hurried over to Edgar's building, surprised to find herself eager to see him. Not an unusual emotion before this whole dating thing started, but since, she'd been a mass of contradictions. Today she felt good, happy, not tied up in knots. Maybe meditating daily was helping. She was following her mom's recommendation to go on the next two dates with Edgar, enjoy herself and worry about deciding what to do later. Maybe a cop-out, but the decision got rid of some of the confusion and most of the stress. For now, anyway.

She pushed the call button to Edgar's apartment, clutching a bottle of wine recommended by the staff at Ray's Liquor on North Avenue. He buzzed her in; she bounded up the two flights and found the door open. Inside, Emma, his cat, lifted her head from the couch pillow, eyed Melanie disdainfully and went back to sleep. The fish ignored her.

Edgar, busy at the stove, paused and flashed her a wide grin. The smile was his customary greeting, but because she now understood the emotions behind it, the welcome made Melanie more and more shivery every time she saw it.

"Hi, Edgar." She held up the wine, a chilled white called Viognier, which she couldn't begin to pronounce. "My contribution."

"Thanks, Mel." He stirred something, checked something else in the oven, then came toward her, wearing a striped canvas apron, which looked at home on him.

"Something smells incredible."

He went to kiss her cheek, and without even thinking, she turned her face toward him so the kiss landed on the corner of her mouth. He lingered the briefest second and she got a small sexual buzz, curious to see what he'd do. He smelled as good as his kitchen, spices and rich roasted smells, and under it his subtle aftershave.

"I hope it will taste good." He took the wine, made appreciative noises after glancing at the label. Not polite noises, but real, as if he understood its quality. He could even pronounce it: *vyon-yeh*.

She felt hopelessly outclassed. By Edgar.

"I'll open it now. White will go well with the soup."

"Mmm, we're having soup?"

"For the first course, yeah."

The *first* course? "What kind?"

"Chilled zucchini with lemon shrimp and cilantro cream."

Her mouth dropped. "Campbell's?"

"Um, no." He laughed and shot her a sexy sidelong look.

Sexy. He was sexy. How had she never noticed? His eyes were incredibly expressive. She must have been asleep for the past two years. Or maybe he was letting her see more than he used to. "Need any help?"

"Open the wine and pour? We can have a glass outside before we eat." He gestured to the back of the kitchen.

"Balcony?" She'd never noticed one.

"Door's right there." He jerked his head to the opposite end of the kitchen where there was a door. "It's small, but nice on summer evenings. It faces the river."

"Sounds perfect." She accepted the corkscrew, managed to get the cork out without making a horrible mess, and poured the wine into elegant crystal glasses that looked delicate enough to shatter from a mere glare. On the narrow balcony he'd set up two chairs and a table on which were bowls of olives, salted nuts and a creamy dip surrounded by cut vegetables. A soft breeze kept the temperature mild; the sun was making its way down behind the buildings across the river to their right, its light gaining in richness what it lost in brightness.

"I had no idea you were such a chef, Edgar."

He shrugged and waited for her to sit before he took the chair next to her. "My parents are into entertaining. I guess I inherited the passion from them."

"What kind of entertaining do they do?"

He blew out a breath. "Mostly impress-other-people entertaining."

"You're hard on them."

He looked surprised, then thoughtful. "You're right, Mel. I should let them be who they are and get over it."

"I didn't mean to criticize."

"No." He swirled his wine in a gesture that looked more like habit than intent. "You're right."

She held out her glass, wanting to take the frown off his face. "I'm honored to be cooked for by you."

"I'm glad." He clinked his glass with hers. "I admit I put special effort into tonight to impress you. So I shouldn't throw stones at Mom and Dad."

She smiled, feeling weirdly shy as she sipped the wine. Not that she had the most educated palate, but it tasted good to her.

"Mmm, that is good wine. Thanks for bringing it."

"You're welcome." She felt absurdly pleased, which was silly because all she'd done was go into Ray's and ask for help.

Except, no, she shouldn't beat herself up; it was more than that. She was pleased because she made Edgar happy, and because she'd added something of quality to the evening.

"Have some?" He offered her the dip, which turned out to be salty and creamy, flavored with dill, and delicious. "Thanks for coming tonight. I know sitting still for an entire evening isn't your thing."

She lifted her chin. "I might become a convert."

He grinned, light slanting across the balcony floor, glinting in his hair. "Of course, we could play party games if you get restless."

"Twister?"

His grin turned wicked. "That might work. Or strip poker."

She laughed, stretched her legs, feeling relaxed and comfortable, enjoying the view, the wine and the company. "This is a great apartment, Edgar."

"It is. But cramped. I'm saving for a house. I should have a down payment in another few months."

"Really?" She blinked at him, wondering why this was such surprising news. "Where will you be looking?"

"Depends. I've been thinking a lot about what I want to do next."

"Next?" She spit out the pit of her olive; he was right there with a small dish to discard it in. "Like what? You're not going to leave Triangle Graphics, are you?"

"I might."

Melanie was aghast. She couldn't imagine coming to work every day without Edgar. It would be dull. Cold. Impersonal. She had Jenny, other friends, but she looked forward to seeing *him*. Her cubicle-mate, her confidant...

A voice inside her whispered that she might have been denying feelings for him for a long, long time.

"I'd like to start my own design business, buy somewhere I could have a first-floor studio-office, around Downer or Brady Streets. I'd also like to go back to school, get my MFA."

"While fencing."

"Of course while fencing."

"That's...wow. You...wow." She sipped her wine while she tried to sort out her thoughts. What were *her* plans? Drinking? Partying? Getting laid? "That's impressive."

"And somewhere in there I want a family."

Melanie nodded, her throat suddenly dry, though he spoke casually. "Me, too. Someday."

She glanced at him. In profile his nose was noble, balanced by the high forehead his new haircut exposed. His jaw was strong, his mouth firm, his eyes lit by the setting sun.

It hit her, an unwelcome thought. Edgar was a man, and she was still an adolescent.

The realization was a shock. She'd spent so long thinking he was a cute, inconsequential geek and she was this great catch, and now she understood in one stunning second that she had it completely backward. He was the great catch; she was an immature fish, suitable only for throwing back. Maybe that was another reason her relationships didn't work out. She was a child expecting serious, committed grown-up results from men who were still children, too.

What plans did she have for her future? How was she contributing to her community besides filling the coffers of bars and clubs? She'd volunteered for a while at Habitat for Humanity—and met Sawyer there, lucky Alana—but she'd done that to meet men. Everything she did was all about her.

"Something wrong?" Edgar was frowning in that puzzled way that endeared him to her so strongly. She'd never met a man—she'd never met anyone, except maybe her mother—who was so tuned in to her emotional changes. Which, face it, were numerous and hard to keep track of, even for her.

"What the hell do you see in me?"

To her surprise, he laughed, put his wineglass down and stared at her thoughtfully. "I have no idea."

"Edgar!"

He laughed again, moved his chair close to hers, put his arm around her and kissed her hair. "Let's see. If I try really hard I might come up with something."

She crossed her arms petulantly across her chest. "Don't strain yourself."

"I don't know…. This could be tough."

She laughed and nudged his shoulder. "I'm not fishing, Edgar, I really want to know. I mean, you have life goals, you're cultured, sophisticated, talented."

"First, on the shallow end, you are beautiful. And sexy."

She forced a modest smile, hiding her fear. She didn't just want to be desired. That might be enough from most guys, but she wanted more from Edgar.

"You have this amazingly energetic and positive life force,

which is incredibly compelling for those of us who sometimes dwell in the valley of insecurity and grumpiness."

A sexy, happy party girl. Was that all? Not the woman he'd want to install in his new house? Just a diversion? Someone to play around with? He said he loved her. Was he mistaking infatuation and fantasy for the real thing, the same way she always did? That was one thing she did *not* want them to have in common.

"Thank you, Edgar." She smiled at him. "That was so sweet. You don't have to keep going. I guess it was more a backhanded compliment on how great you are than a real need to hear my qualities."

His eyes narrowed. "What am I missing?"

"What?"

"Something's bugging you."

She laughed uneasily. How did he do that? She could hide nothing from him. "No, nothing."

"Uh-huh." He took her wine, put it on the table, held both of her hands in his. His fingers were long and strong, well-formed. "I'm missing the deep end."

"What do you mean?"

"You already know I think you're incredibly hot. You want to know why I love you, and I'm not sure I can tell you that exactly. We have the same sense of humor, the same values. Some of the rest is bound up in this caveman need to save you from yourself, and I know that probably sounds macho and stupid."

"No, I understand. Unfortunately."

"But I think it has more to do with this spirit in you that I don't think you're aware you have. I don't mean to sound condescending again, but I think you…are destined for things you haven't tried yet." He broke off in frustration. "I don't know how to say this. I think we have more in common than it might seem on the surface. There is a lot of depth to you, certainly a lot of intelligence. I want at it. Because I think we can grow together in the same direction. And that's what makes relationships succeed."

His intensity started her heart pounding, both in pleasure and fear. He understood her, maybe better than she did—at least until she started paying attention. He was incredible. And he'd been right under her nose for two years.

She put on a deliberately innocent face. "So...you're saying you want into my depths?"

"Oh, Mel." He grinned, his eyes darkening. "You know I do."

She widened her eyes in faux shock. "Right now?"

His eyebrow lifted; his grin turned devilish. "We don't have to worry about the soup getting cold."

"Well." She giggled, and an evil thought struck her. They were facing the river, which curved around his building, heading southwest to east. Who would see them?

She gasped and pointed down at the water through the balcony railing bars as if she'd just seen something extraordinary. "Look! Look right there, on the river. That bird! What's it doing?"

He stood, leaned over the railing, searching earnestly. She whipped off her shirt, laid it gently on the floor.

"Where?"

"Right there, by that...black thing." She unhooked her bra, let it drop, picked up her glass and sat nonchalantly back in her seat, feeling the breeze caressing her breasts, tightening her nipples.

"I don't see..."

"Maybe it flew away." She turned her face to the sun and sipped her wine, out of her peripheral vision catching him turning back toward her.

"Yeah, may—" He froze as if he'd been zapped. "Melanie."

"Mmm?" She tilted her head, sent him a look. "Anything wrong? You look kind of...stiff."

He passed his hand over his eyes as if he couldn't trust them. "I think I just came down with something. Or rather... up with something."

She stood, came close to him, a breeze pushing her hair to catch briefly on his lips, breasts brushing the soft cotton of his shirt. "Maybe you better sit down."

"Out here?" He moved backward under the pressure of her hand on his chest. She could feel the developed pectoral muscles under her fingers, and her sexual temperature started rising.

"Yes. Out here."

He sat, staring at her hungrily, amusement lurking in his eyes. "I'm in for it, aren't I?"

"Oh, you have no idea." She brought her hands to the back of her neck, lifted her hair and arched toward him, then brought one hand down over her face, her lips parted by her descending fingers.

"I'm in for it," he whispered.

She covered her breasts with her hands, touched them for him, offering them to him, one by one without moving closer.

Edgar shifted in his chair, adjusted his fly, cleared his throat. "I think this might kill me."

"I hope not."

She put her hands to the waistband of her bright blue skirt, edged it down, swinging her hips in opposition to the motion, rocking down, right and left and right and left, until it cleared her hips and slid to the floor. She'd worn thong underwear, since the skirt clung in back, and was glad of it now.

"No, you don't understand, this is *definitely* going to kill me."

"Oh, what a shame." She turned her back to him, undulating her ass, twisting so she could look at his face. One by one she put her fingers into her mouth, sucking each, tasting olive, salt, wine and anticipation.

"Mel..." He groaned and unzipped his shorts, brought his erection out and started stroking. "I think I'm going to lose it."

"Let me help you." She stepped between his legs; he leaned forward and kissed her stomach, slipping his free hand around, moving his fingers lightly over her exposed rear, following the material of the thong down between her buttocks.

She moved one leg, straddling him, then the other, preparing to lower herself. "Condom?"

"Not out here. I can go inside and—"

"No." She hated interrupting the spontaneous flow of arousal. "We'll do without."

"Melanie, I'm not going to—"

"Shhh." She shook her head. "No risks. Just watch."

She sank down slowly, carefully, until she was sitting on his lap, his cock lying hot and hard against the small strip of her panties.

"Now." She braced her feet on the chair's side rails and started to move, up and down, stroking his erection, while its hard length rubbed her clitoris through her panties. The friction was indirect, hot, tantalizing. She lifted his cock against her, palmed its other side, lifted to cup his balls underneath her, then slid back down again. "How's this?"

"Ohh, it'll work." He was breathing hard, watching her sliding against his penis, his hands on her waist, helping support her. Always helping, always taking some of the burden onto himself. An extraordinary man.

He leaned forward, caught her breast in his mouth, sucked hard, pinching her nipple with his teeth.

"Mmm." She quickened her rhythm, legs starting to tremble, but unable to stop craving the thrust of that hard heat between them.

He left that breast, which turned cool with damp in the breeze; his warm mouth started on the other while his hand found the back of her thong and pulled rhythmically, sending the material deeper into her, tightening its pressure against her sex.

She started panting, the world became blurry around her, her senses focused on the contact between them, on the strong muscles of his arm against her back, on the need to climax and to have him with her when she did.

"Later," she whispered. "After dinner, inside, in your room, I want you to blindfold me and tie my hands and feet to the bed, spread-eagle, facedown, with pillows under my stomach lifting my ass so I'm naked and spread open to you. I want you to make me wait, doing nothing, just having me lie there with the air licking and stroking me while I imagine you doing the same.

"Then I want you to silently touch me, fingers, feet, tongue—slap, tickle, pinch, bite, caress—whatever you want to do to me, just so I don't know when the next touch will come from, how you'll want to give it to me. Then I want you to kneel behind me and tease me with the head of your cock, but not give it to me yet, not yet, not until I'm begging you, Eddie."

"Melanie," he whispered hoarsely. "You're going to make me come."

"Yes, yes, go." She was so worked up she wouldn't be far behind. "Because there's more. When I'm there, helpless, tied up with my ass in the air, I want you to be like a fencer, make a sudden attack, lunge and thrust, give it to me hard until I'm pleading with you, please, to make me come."

She could barely speak, rubbing herself up and down on him, cheeks hot, body shaking, orgasm building. She had to hold on. "But don't let me come, Eddie, not until I'm so hot for you I'm nearly crying. Not until I promise I'll do whatever you want with whatever part of my body you want me to do it with, and then make me do that as many times as you want."

He gripped her hard, took in breath harshly; she rode him

a few more times and allowed herself to let go. At the peak of her climax he looked up and she sank into his beautiful blue eyes, feeling him contract and go over, the wetness spreading between them.

She couldn't look away. They sat there she didn't know how long, eyes locked, sharing everything, holding nothing back.

"Melanie," he whispered. "I love you."

She nodded. She couldn't answer out loud, but she knew he didn't expect her to. She knew this incredible man would keep giving and giving whether she ever managed to give back or not.

And that made her finally realize what she must have known for a long time but had been too scared to admit.

Edgar, I love you, too.

14

Melanie sat at The Wicked Hop, waiting for Stoner. Same bar where she'd waited for him a week and a half earlier, but it was hard to imagine different emotions. He'd called, asking her to meet him, but without anything more than mild flirting that sounded like habit. He'd seemed distracted, unsure of himself, not the Stoner she knew. Not her fantasy, anyway.

She grinned at the thought. Quite a few aspects of her previous behavior with men were coming clear to her. Slowly. She wasn't going to change overnight, but she could at least commit to dating Edgar, one day at a time. Yes, she was nervous, yes, she was wary, but the emotions she felt when she was with him, the easy way they were together, his kindness, his undeniable talent in the bedroom

"Hey, Mel-a-nie." Stoner clapped her on the shoulder, nearly toppling her off the bar stool. "Sorry I'm late. Rehearsal ran late. How's it going, babe?"

"Fine." She smiled, thinking how grateful she was that Edgar never called her "babe." "How's the performing going? You're heading on soon, aren't you?"

"Yeah. Yeah. Had a concert in Fort Atkinson Saturday, but we're about done." He leaned on the bar, rubbing his hands together. "Heading on...yeah, I guess."

The bartender came over; Stoner ordered a double shot of tequila.

"You guess?" She was mystified. Not that she knew him well, but every time she'd seen him, he'd been ultrasmooth and drank only beer.

"I, uh, called because I wanted to talk to you."

"Okay." She started getting a bad feeling. Was this going to be something about her and Edgar? A skeleton in the closet? Or some objection from Stoner? His family? Or God forbid, was he going to come on to her now, one of those guys who didn't want women until they didn't want him? Though she was not getting a sex vibe from him. "What's up?"

"I need some advice."

Melanie blinked. Advice from her? What could Stoner possibly—

"It's about a girl. A *woman*." He grinned at her with those beautiful blue eyes. Funny how all she saw in him now was a lesser version of Edgar.

"Ah, okay." She felt somewhat relieved. This would be easier than anything she'd been imagining. "What's the problem?"

"I think she likes me. I do. But, um, I keep messing up, and I'm not used to that. I'd talk to Edgar, but man, you know, it's like guys don't admit that shit to each other."

"Messing up how?"

"Like, I asked her if she wanted to go out. And she looked all excited. But then I said she could come watch me play and she was all like, um, I'm busy that night."

"And you don't think she was?"

"No, man, I don't."

Melanie grinned. How many times had she gone out with guys like this? How had she ever put up with it? At least this woman had more sense than she did. "Okay, I do have one idea."

"Yeah?" He looked so hopeful she was actually touched.

"Maybe she'd like to do something…" Melanie paused, not sure how to say "something that doesn't involve admiring you all night" without offending him. "Something that involves her more. I mean, where you could get to know her. That might be more fun for you, too. It's kind of hard to talk in those loud places."

She heard herself and nearly burst out laughing. Why hadn't she had this talk with herself, oh, say, about ten years ago? She wouldn't have listened. The evolution of Melanie.

"Damn, you are sounding just like my brother." Stoner downed his tequila, slammed the glass on the bar.

"Who is this woman?"

"Kaitlin. From the coffee shop."

"Kaitlin?" Melanie gaped at him. "Edgar's Kaitlin?"

"Not Edgar's," he said testily. "Yeah, the one that works at Caffe Coffee. I don't know, it's like I went in there because he told me she brews a great cup, and I walk in and introduce myself and it's like…I don't know, ton of bricks I guess."

"This isn't like you?"

"Well, I mean, I like the ladies. I really do. Give me a hot woman and I'm all over it. Like you, for instance. You are a total babe, Mel-a-nie."

She grinned. Thank God she'd never, ever started anything with this charming cretin. "Thanks, Stoner. You're pretty much of a babe yourself."

"Thanks. Thanks a lot. This woman is like…" He thumped his chest. "In here. Like a disease, you know, like flesh-eating bacteria, eating me up."

She wrinkled her nose. "Almost Shakespearean."

"Yeah, maybe I won't use that one again. But you know what I mean, right?"

"Yeah." She took a sip of her beer, thinking of Edgar.

"Yeah. Yeah, you got it, right there." He pointed to her face. "That stupid faraway look like you've lost your mind. That's exactly how I feel all day. I hate it."

She laughed hard enough to get tears in her eyes. "It's not that bad once you give in."

"Oh, man, you sound like Satan. Sell your soul to me and all will be well."

"Go for it, Stoner." She nudged him affectionately with her shoulder.

"Yeah, I guess. I guess. So you think offering to watch me play is the problem?"

"Yeah." She put her hand on his arm. "I do. Take her somewhere nice, somewhere quiet, maybe a picnic at the—"

"A *picnic?!*" He opened his mouth in comical horror. "With a barbecue, maybe, so I can cut off my balls and grill them for her?"

Melanie barely managed to keep beer from going up her nose. *"Stoner."*

"I know, over the top." He shook his head, signaled to the bartender and held up his empty tequila glass. "I think I get what you're saying."

"Just ask what *she'd* like to do. She might surprise you."

"You mean like maybe she's not into picnics? That would work."

"Maybe she is, maybe not. Maybe she'll suggest going to an S and M swingers club."

"Whoa." His eyes popped. Then he smiled that great not-quite-Edgar smile. "You know, I can see why my brother is in love with you. Sorry we never managed to hook up. But once I found out about you and him, whoa. I'm not going there, not on my own brother."

"You're a good guy, Stoner. I hope Kaitlin gets to see that."

"Oh, man, even her name gets me all churned up." He laughed nervously. "I'll ask her out again. I'll go by there tomorrow morning right when the shop opens."

"Isn't that like at 7:00 a.m.?"

"Can you believe it? I've got it bad." He shook his head and winked at her. "Just like Edgar."

"Good luck, Stoner. And remember this. It sounds weird, but you have to trust me, because I just lived it for the first time. With the right person even a picnic can surprise you." She held up her mug and clinked it with his shot glass, giddy with certainty that she'd just freed herself from men like Stoner for the rest of her life. "What's more, with the right person, you can even surprise yourself."

EDGAR SALUTED HIS imaginary opponent. *En garde. Allez.*

Attack, balestra, lunge, parry, counterriposte, *ha! Got the bastard.*

He was breathing hard, body tense, puncturing his enemy repeatedly on the balcony of his apartment, which was by now awash with imaginary blood. The air was humid, though the temperature wasn't high enough for air-conditioning, and he was sweating like a pig.

Stoner was out with Melanie.

Balestra, lunge, parry, counterriposte, *ha! Sucker fell for it every time.*

Generally when he practiced, Edgar fell into a high of concentration, body alert, mind clear and attuned to the smallest detail, all qualities he'd need to react instantaneously to his opponent, make split-second decisions regarding defense moves and subsequent attacks. There were moments when he felt he knew what his opponent was going to do before he did it.

However, in the case of Melanie, he didn't have that luxury. So far he'd made more progress with her, had her responding to him and opening up about her feelings more than he'd ever dared imagine.

Okay, scratch that, he imagined it every day.

Balestra, lunge, parry, counterriposte, again, *yes! Death to the unknown foe.*

Today his form was fine, but his mind kept going off in different directions. Were Melanie and Stoner having fun? How much fun? For how long? Where? In what position?

He trusted her, and for a change he trusted his brother, but…his relationship with Melanie was still so new, so tentative, at least for her. They'd come further faster than he'd hoped, but knowing Melanie, she was liable to bolt at the slightest unexpected turn. Part of her charm was the enthusiasm with which she threw herself into new situations, relationships, opportunities.

Balestra, flèche—bolting past his opponent to avoid a riposte, and he was ready to hit the shower. He'd been practicing at the club, then out here over an hour, needing action to work out his frustration and worry.

But right now he was exhausted.

He trudged into his bathroom, turned on the shower and stripped.

Stoner wasn't a bad person. And he seemed genuinely smitten with Kaitlin, though who knew how she felt. But Stoner liked to drink, and he liked women, and his ego seemed to need a steady supply of both or he got moody and depressed. Even when they were kids he'd always been about impressing the opposite sex. Who knew where he got it? Maybe their weird uncle Chad, Mom's brother. Dad was attractive, but cerebral, a take-charge hard worker, a strong authority figure, but not what Edgar would call a passionate guy. Edgar took after their interior-decorator mother, more of an observer, a peacemaker with strong empathy and her own brand of obstinacy.

He glanced at his watch. Ten. They'd met at eight. He took off his watch and tossed it onto the top of the hamper in disgust. *Stop, Edgar.*

In the shower, he lathered and scrubbed off the sweat, trying not to think of them together, trying not to think of what they might be doing, of Stoner touching the beautiful body he'd been crazy enough already to imagine was his. Melanie touching another man—

Was that the phone? His eyes shot open; he yanked off the water and ripped back the curtain.

Yes.

He stepped out of the tub; his foot slipped and he went down hard on his hip, wrenching his arm as he tried to stop his fall.

Ow.

The pain peaked, subsided. He wasn't badly hurt. The phone had stopped ringing.

Edgar got up, breathing hard, heart pounding even harder, checking his joints and bones mentally. Bruises maybe, that was all. He could have killed himself. Knocked his head against the sink or the tub rim. Most accidents happened in the bathroom, yada yada.

All because he was imagining something that probably wasn't even happening.

Why wasn't he imagining the way she looked after she climaxed with him out on the balcony, before they came inside, ate dinner, pulled out a supply of condoms and continued the party all night?

Why wasn't he imagining the way she was with him in the shower the next morning, soft and warm and naked and wet? She'd taken him into her mouth so sweetly, kneeling on the tub floor, water beading and running off her face, her hair slicked back tight to her scalp.

Whoa. Seriously. Why?

He stretched, worked his arm, rotating his shoulder joint, moving his elbow forward and back. No serious injury there, either.

He was a lucky guy. A lucky guy in a lot of ways. The most amazing beautiful girl in the world could be falling in love with him and all he could think about was how it could go wrong, how he could be wrong for her, how he might not be enough.

What the hell? Time to reorder that thinking. Time to trust her, to trust what they had together, and to trust that he was worth it.

The phone rang again. He took his time getting there. Melanie's cell. "Hello?"

"Hey." Her voice was low, soft and intimate.

"Melanie, hi, how's it going?"

"Just had an interesting talk with your brother."

"Oh, yeah?" He tried to sound casual, almost succeeded.

"Remember how you told me I had three dates to decide if I wanted to be with you?"

"Mmm, yeah." His voice was gravelly with nerves.

"I should have told you last time."

His swallow was audible. "Yeah?"

"It only took me one date to know."

Silence. He was paralyzed with fear, wanting the right answer so badly that he couldn't even speak.

"Edgar?"

"Yuh?"

"You're not...I mean you're not happy?"

"Happy?" He went back over her words. She hadn't said anything happy. "You said you made your decision."

"Yes."

"Um, Melanie?"

"Mmm?"

"You forgot to mention what that decision was."

She gasped. "No way. I did? Sorry, I'm a little drunk."

"Melanie."

She giggled. "I can't believe I led you right up to the payoff like that and didn't deliver. Jeez."

"Melanie." He was grinning, nearly overflowing, like a joy balloon was slowly inflating in his chest. Two years he'd fantasized about this moment. Two years. Now he had his

answer. It hadn't sunk in yet, but he had it. He just wanted to hear the words right from between her gorgeous lips. "Say it."

"It's you, Edgar. I want to be with you." Her voice was low and breathy. His cock responded as if she were an X-rated video. He turned toward the door, imagining her standing there already. Naked. Smiling. His.

"Then why don't you come over right now?"

MELANIE CLINKED THE SIDE of her glass with her fork to get attention, a completely unnecessary gesture in Tricia's opinion, since she and Alana were less than an elbow's length away, having breakfast at Ted's Diner.

"I know you're wondering why I've brought us together today."

Alana lifted an eyebrow. "To have breakfast?"

"I wasn't actually wondering, Melanie, no." Tricia winked at Alana, who smiled. A little stiffly, but she did smile.

Melanie made a sound of acute exasperation. "Come on, how often do I actually want to go out to breakfast before work?"

"When you're still up from the night before?" Alana sipped her coffee innocently.

"I'm not still up from—" Melanie rested her forehead on her hand in defeat, unable to control a smile. She was radiant. Glowing. So lovely. Of course, Tricia thought that about her daughters all the time. She didn't deserve such perfect offspring, but thank God for both of them.

"Hey, Melanie." Tricia sipped her coffee nonchalantly. "I was wondering something. Seriously."

"What's that?"

"*Why* did you bring us together this morning?"

"You know, I was wondering that *exact* same thing." Alana shook her head in awe. "Whoa. It's like we're related."

Tricia laughed and patted Melanie's hand. "Have we driven you crazy enough or shall we keep going?"

"Oh, by all means, keep going. I don't think I'm quite insane enough yet." She put a finger gun to her temple.

"So...?"

"So what?" Melanie blinked, then held up her hands. "Okay. I have an official announcement."

"Oh, my God, you're engaged." Alana thumped a hand to her chest.

Tricia's heart started pounding. God, not to Stoner. Melanie had gone out with him the night before and—

"No. No. God, no. Not." Melanie made earnest denial motions, waving both hands at them. "Don't give me a heart attack."

"Give *you* a heart attack?" Tricia put down her cup. She didn't need more caffeine until her pulse calmed down.

"Sorry, I jumped the gun." Alana peered at her sister curiously. "What is it?"

"As much as it pains me intensely to admit it, you were right." She looked from mother to sister. "Both of you."

"About..." Alana beckoned encouragingly.

"Stoner."

"Whew." Alana fanned herself. "Thank God. And yes, we certainly were."

"*And* about..." She started blushing. "Edgar."

"Edgar!" Tricia exchanged a glance with Alana and held up her hand for a high five, which Alana actually gave her. "You're dating him?"

"For real?"

"Yes. Yes." Melanie nodded. "He's...he's just... He's so..."

Her eyes filled with tears.

Alana's jaw dropped. "Oh, my God. Melanie."

"What?" She looked at her sister, eyes shining, lip trembling.

"You're in love. I mean really." She put her hand on top of her sister's and squeezed, her own eyes filling up.

Which meant a lump the size of Rhode Island formed in Tricia's throat, watching the affection between her girls. Maybe her neglect had helped that bond thrive. Maybe. Silver linings were hard to find.

"Yeah, I think I really am." Melanie laughed breathlessly. "Finally."

"Isn't it amazing? And scary? And fabulous?"

"All of the above."

"I'm so happy for you, sweetie. You so deserve this." Alana's voice trembled; her hand was white-knuckled, squeezing her sister's.

Tricia was nearly overcome. "Alana, I have never seen you look as beautiful as you do now."

Alana looked startled, turned to her mother. Their eyes met for a long time, one pair brown, one blue. "Thanks, Mom."

Mom.

Tears rose; she couldn't help it. And why not? Bawling seemed to be the order of the morning.

"My God, will you look at the three of us?" Melanie laughed, wiping her tears. "Complete basket cases."

"Excuse me." Alana signaled the waitress. "More coffee for the hormonal trio here."

The waitress grinned and brought over the pot. "Happy tears?"

"Oh, yes."

"Good stuff." While they blew noses and wiped eyes, she splashed coffee into each of their cups, then left, smiling.

"Whew." Alana tucked her tissue into her sleeve, giving Tricia a jolt of recognition. Her mom did that. "What's next? When will you see Edgar again?"

"He's taking me to hear the Chicago Symphony at Ravinia this Friday."

"Holy crap, *you* are going to hear a *symphony* concert?"

"And I used to think loud and crowded was the only way to have a good time." Melanie picked up her coffee cup and shrugged. "Edgar is showing me another world. Actually... he's showing me another me."

Something clicked in Tricia's brain, making her think of Jim. Of course, she might as well face it, she was always thinking of Jim. They'd gotten together a couple of times since visiting Beatrice, once for a hike, once for lunch, but he called or e-mailed every day. She was getting used to having him in her life, and wasn't sure what to do about it.

"This is good. Really good. Sawyer showed me a new me, too." Alana grinned approvingly, then leaned forward and nudged her sister with her elbow. "How is Edgar in the, um, you know..."

"Spectacular. Best ever." Stars were practically shooting out the top of her head.

"Because he *cares* about you," Alana said. "That's sort of how it's supposed to work."

"Yeah." Melanie twisted her mouth wryly. "Go figure."

Tricia bit her lip, remembering her crazy passion with Jim in the van, how different it had felt. She'd assumed it was because she was actually in full possession of her senses for a change. But maybe it was because, like Edgar, Jim was a good guy who cared about her.

"Mom, you're the only one single now," Alana said.

Tricia straightened abruptly. "As it should be. I'm taking a long overdue break from men."

"Oh, yeah?" Alana sent her sister a sly look. "What's up with this Jim guy?"

"Jim?" She shrugged. "He's just a friend."

"Really?" Melanie shot Alana a look back. "Tell us more about him, Mom."

"Well, he's a photographer. He has a studio on Brady Street."

"But what's he like?" Melanie asked. "Is he good to you?"

"Oh, well, he's..." Her throat thickened. "He's very... kind."

"And?" Alana dropped her chin into her hand, stared relentlessly.

"And...and thoughtful." Her voice cracked bizarrely.

"Really. And?" Melanie's turn, looking smug.

"Very...support've..." Her voice trailed away in tears.

Melanie and Alana burst out laughing.

"Mom, you are so busted," Melanie said.

"No, no." She shook her head adamantly. "It's not like that. We've been friends for so long, we go way back, it's just...I can't get involved now, this is my for-me time, and besides, I'm leaving, and—"

"Excuses, excuses." Alana waved them away. "You're hit, too."

"Welcome to the club, Mom."

"You're in it, might as well accept your fate."

Tricia grinned at her daughters, overwhelmed by the bliss of being part of a real family, one she no longer took the slightest bit for granted. One she hardly felt she deserved.

"I can't tell you what a privilege and pleasure it is to belong—" she reached, took their hands and squeezed, profoundly grateful for this second chance "—to any club that has both of you as members."

15

NOT SINCE THE BEGINNING of time had there been a more perfect day. Edgar was sure of it. And the best was still to come.

He'd picked a night when the Chicago Symphony was playing an all-Tchaikovsky program, figuring the rich romantic music would set the perfect mood. He'd packed a picnic—cold oven-fried chicken, parmesan sesame biscuits, a fruit-and-greens salad with mint—and picked Melanie up—miraculously she was ready on time. The drive was uneventful, traffic moving, the air soft and warm, humidity low.

They lay together out on the lawn behind the music shed, eating and listening, talking and listening some more. She was more beautiful and more peaceful than he'd ever seen her. He had no idea how he kept from making love to her right there on the blanket. Maybe the threat of jail had something to do with it, but he was tempted nonetheless.

He wanted to stand up and shout to the world that she was his, that he'd won her, like knights of old battling dragons, armies and wicked witches to claim their true loves.

Okay, he was ridiculous. But that's how it felt. He swore he was taller, the air was cleaner, the colors around him more vivid.

They talked and talked, kissed, held hands, kissed some more. And now they were pulling up in front of his apartment, where surprise champagne and strawberry shortcake waited, along with a gift he'd bought her misguidedly weeks ago and was now ready to give her.

"Edgar, what a wonderful evening. Thank you."

"It's not over yet." He tried not to sound too excited.

"Mmm, no?" She got out and waggled her eyebrows over the top of the car at him. If he lived to be a thousand, he would never stop thinking she was the sexiest woman in the world.

"No." He grinned at her, hauled the picnic things out of the car and took her hand. *Home.* What wouldn't he give for a guarantee they'd have one together someday?

At his apartment, he unlocked the door, shoved it open and gestured her inside. Stoner had waited for Edgar to ring his cell when they were about ten minutes away, then he'd lit candles and put the food out as Edgar asked him to, and snuck out of the apartment to spend the night with his new love, Kaitlin. The rest Edgar had prepared before he left to pick Melanie up.

"Edgar." She stood with her hands clasped, eyes shining in the candlelight. "This is amazing. How did you manage it?"

"I'm magic, didn't you know? Hogwarts class of '95."

A white bowl of red strawberries stood next to the silver tray of shortcake biscuits. A bowl of whipped cream with a silver ladle sat next to that. A jet-black ice bucket holding a frosty bottle of champagne and two crystal flutes completed the dessert feast.

"You spoil me." She was so pleased she sounded breathless. And he'd done so little.

"You deserve spoiling, Melanie. You haven't been enough. Certainly not by the men you dated, and your grandparents sounded pretty strict."

"They were. Loving, but yes." Tears glistened in her eyes. She threw her arms around his neck and kissed him.

He enveloped her and rocked her gently, still unable to believe he could now hold her like this, and have it mean something to both of them. "Hungry for dessert?"

"Hungry for you."

"How about both?" He led her to the table. "We can feed each other in bed and make a complete mess."

"I like the sound of that." She laughed and stretched, reaching her arms up into the air, making him want to toss her over his shoulder and ravish her, cavemanlike in the bedroom. "I can't believe how contented I feel. And relaxed. What a great day this has been."

"We'll make sure it doesn't end soon."

He served them strawberry shortcake and champagne; they took it into his bedroom, stripped to their underwear and shirts and sat side by side under the sheets, sipping bubbly and spooning shortcake into each other's mouths between strawberry-and-cream kisses. Edgar was sure he'd never been this content, either.

Until she spilled a strawberry on her chest and took the shirt off, rubbed it clean in the bathroom and came back without one on.

Then he was no longer content. In fact, he had a very specific idea of what was missing. And once she got a look at the sheet over his lap she figured it out quickly, too.

"One thing first." He put his champagne flute on the bedside table and reached over the edge for the package he'd been saving.

"What's this?"

"I think you'll recognize it."

She frowned. "I didn't get you anything."

"Why would you? This is spoiling. Get used to it."

"Yes, *sir.*" She giggled and started tearing off the paper, her curious expression relaxing into pleasure when the necklace came into view. "Oh, Edgar."

"You remember?"

She held up the beautiful piece she'd picked out purportedly for Edgar's "girlfriend." He'd so desperately wanted her to have it, and his fantasy had been strong enough to think someday he'd have a moment like this when he could give it to her for real. The deception seemed so childish and embarrassing now.

Melanie had changed him.

"Of course I remember. It's so beautiful!" She pushed aside her hair; he leaned over to help her put it on, remembering how much he'd wanted to kiss her exposed neck in Sledge's apartment the first time he put it on her, how much he still did. ...

"How does it look?"

He just stared, shaking his head. "Like it was made for you. You're beautiful."

"Stop." She made a face that didn't hide her pleasure. "Stop, I'm serious, you're going to give me a huge head."

"No, you're giving *me* a huge —"

"Stop that, perv boy." She whacked him gently on the shoulder. "I was thinking about the day I picked this out."

"Yeah?" He rubbed his shoulder, pretending serious pain.

"I think that was the first day I got a clue how you felt about me."

He groaned. "I was so lame. For all I knew at the time I could have been doomed to keep the necklace for the rest of my life. To sleep with it under my pillow, drooling, until I was a hundred years old. 'Mel-uh-neee.'"

She cracked up at his old-man whine. "See, you didn't have to."

"No." He sobered some, telling her with his eyes what was in his heart. "I didn't have to."

"It's perfect." She leaned forward; the necklace dangled over her breasts, which were calling to his hands and mouth.

"Mmm, perfect." He kissed her over and over, then eased her down onto the mattress, helped her off with her underpants and bra, and then let her help him off with his boxers. Being with her felt so natural and so right. It had from the beginning. This was forever for him. Forever.

And when he slid inside her, gently tonight, reverently, he knew he'd never feel this way about anyone else.

"I love you, Melanie."

She clung to him, arched to his rhythm, her movements as languorous and unhurried as his. There was no need to hurry. They had all night. All tomorrow. All the next day and the next.

"I love you, too, Edgar. I always have. I'm sorry it took me so long to realize. I fought who I was for so long, I was so into this idea of being a wild woman like my mother, and I was just scared. I'm not afraid anymore. Because of you."

His heart stopped. His body stopped, too, but only for a moment. Then joy rushed through him so fiercely he could barely keep from howling it to the moon like a wolf.

She deserved a response, but he was too overwhelmed to trust speech, so he made love to her every way that showed her what he couldn't say; she kept pace, shifting to accommodate him, always matching his hunger and his mood.

He held back so they came at the same time, staring into each other's eyes, and he knew with a solid, deep certainty that this was what he'd dreamed of for two years, and that there was no reason to wait any longer.

"Melanie." He gathered her to him. The hugeness of the moment made his voice solemn and a little shaky.

"Mmm, yes?"

"You said you're not afraid anymore."

"No." She kissed his shoulder, fitted herself to him. "Not at all."

"I want to ask you something."

"Sure." She put her hand to his chest, totally relaxed, stroked him, collarbone to belly, shoulder to shoulder. "I'm your open book now. Ask whatever you want."

"Okay." He took a deep breath, feeling like a bungee jumper standing on the edge of a bridge. "Melanie. Will you marry me?"

16

ALL THE WAY TO JIM's place on Brady Street Tricia repeated her resolution. *I am not in love. Jim is a friend.*

Okay, a close friend.

She'd given the matter a lot of thought since talking it over at Ted's with her girls. She'd meditated once or twice, but her inner voice had nothing to say, which had been incredibly frustrating, but also a relief, because if it told her to be with Jim, she'd have an entire life's philosophy to rethink. Again.

There was so much to be thankful for right now. Sobriety, independence, a good relationship with her family—both her daughters and her parents. Her painting gave her a lot of joy, and someday she hoped it would make her money, too. In the meantime, she'd landed a job in a salon on Blue Mound Road, so she could be financially independent while she was here.

It was most important to stay powerful and whole. As she'd realized on the cliff at Devil's Lake, if she got in deep with Jim, she'd be dependent again on a man for her happiness. She so desperately wanted to make her own happiness first, and *then* find a man to share it.

Not yet, though. Not so soon after reclaiming her sanity

and her strength. She needed to grow solid on her own two feet.

She parked in front of Jim's studio and walked determinedly up to the door, rang and held herself straight, tall, chin lifted, wishing her mental recitation of the be-strong philosophy didn't feel like such upstream effort.

The door opened.

Tricia managed a friendly smile, but her heart started pounding. Damn it.

"Hi." The word was simple, but he managed to make it clear that in this case "hi" meant *God, I am so glad to see you.*

Steady, Tricia.

"Hi, Jim. How's it going?" Her voice was too cheerful. She sounded like a TV-commercial mom extolling the virtues of some laundry detergent.

"Fine." He smiled and his eyes crinkled deliciously in the corners. "You look stunning."

"Oh." She had taken great pains with her appearance to look as if she hadn't taken great pains with her appearance. She was wearing a knee-length blue knit skirt and a white top with thin black, red and blue horizontal stripes. Something she might wear to go shopping, read in her backyard, something casual. Nothing meaningful and carrying possibly tremendous significance for the rest of her life. Nothing like that. "Thanks. It's comfortable."

"That's good." He ushered her inside and up the stairs to his apartment, looking at her in that quirked-eyebrow way that said he hadn't figured her mood out yet, but had no doubt he would.

"Jim, your place is fabulous." Tricia stopped convincing herself she wasn't in love with him long enough to realize she was in love with his apartment. He collected African and Indian art; the place was a riot of color and atmosphere, ebony

busts and elephant tapestries, masks and drums and statues
of Buddha. "Did you collect these here or on travels?"

"All here so far. It's a hobby of mine. Maybe an obsession.
Someday I'm going to travel. When I retire. Meanwhile, business keeps me pretty busy."

"I can imagine." Tricia fingered a fierce-looking feathered
mask, feeling strangely hollow and wistful. She envied his
plans, his stability, his smart choices. She'd be working for the
rest of her life to make up for all those years without saving.
So stupid. So shortsighted.

No regrets.

"I thought we could have a drink here before dinner. I'd
love to show you my studio."

"I'd love to see it."

"Virgin mojito? Also known as a mint lime spritzer?"

She turned from the mask. "Did you, Jim Francis Bronson,
just offer me a *spritzer?*"

"It's true." He shook his head sadly. "We all give up our
youthful principles sooner or later. It's a good drink. Refreshing. You can pretend there's rum in it."

"I'm sure it's delicious. I just had to tease you."

His eyes took on an intensity that made her want to step
back and run toward him at the same time. "You can tease
me anytime you want, Tee."

"Well. Thank you," she said oh-so-primly. Jim winked,
then went toward his kitchen to make the drinks. Unable to
resist, she trailed after him.

"How are the girls?" He took a pitcher out of the refrigerator. She noticed it was packed with real food, not like the
refrigerator he'd had in the apartment with Tom, which held...
beer.

"Great. Both in love. Melanie is down at Ravinia tonight
with Edgar, and Alana is having dinner with Sawyer at Sanford Restaurant."

"Beautiful music, Milwaukee's best food. They've got men

with good taste." He poured two glasses, then got out a small bottle of seltzer. "How are things going with you and Alana? Still good?"

Tricia went to examine a bronze statue of a four-armed dancing Shiva on his counter, a representation of good triumphing over evil. "After that breakthrough at Ted's, yes. We're up to her calling me Mom five times."

"Now that's progress." He handed her a glass, smiling warmly—her joys made him happy—then lifted his in a toast. "Here's to you getting your family back, Tee."

"Thank you." She had to glance away when she drank. The intimacy between them was so powerful just looking into his eyes made her want to touch him. Everywhere.

"Come downstairs. We'll prowl around together."

"Deal." She followed him, glad for a change of scene. Being with Jim in his home, loving that home…it all felt too domestic. And too natural.

His studio was neatly kept, attractive, with potted plants by the storefront window; she lingered over the colorful portraits and landscapes on the walls, all done with great skill. He was very talented.

"This way. I want to show you something."

She followed again, thinking how often he'd said he wanted to show her something in the short time she'd known him again. Thinking how Melanie talked about Edgar, how Alana talked about Sawyer, showing them new things, showing them new selves.

She could be in some serious trouble here.

He led her into a backroom office and handed her a folder.

"What's this?"

"A present. Open it."

She frowned at him, then opened it and found herself staring at herself, perched on a cliff at Devil's Lake. "Jim."

The picture was beautiful. Maybe Photoshop was

responsible, but she didn't think she'd looked that good in years. Or maybe ever, since she'd been so hard on her body most of her adult life.

"What do you think?"

"I look so..." She frowned, trying to put into words what he'd captured. A side of her she thought she no longer had. Or maybe her new self. Peaceful, grounded, untarnished. Looking off to the left of the photographer as if she saw great things ahead and was confident they'd come to her.

"You look the way you are. I don't think you truly see yourself."

He was standing too close. Much too close. She took a step back and he followed. "There is so much more to you than you allow yourself to believe. Those drawings? They're great. Beatrice went nuts over them. I talked to her again yesterday. She said you had a unique style that would jump out at the reader, that your faces were so full of life she could read any and every emotion into them."

Tricia took a sip of her drink, clutching the glass too hard. "That was very sweet."

"She wasn't being nice. She was expressing a professional opinion."

Much, much too close. She could catch his scent. Everything in her wanted to turn and wrap her arms around him. It had been too long. She was lonely. It could happen with any man, this need for physical contact. She had always needed more than most people, and it had been a while.

Nope. She wasn't buying it, either.

"I wanted to show you yourself as I see you, as you are. Because I don't think you see that woman very often."

"Jim..." She could barely breathe. He was giving her everything she needed right now. Pride in her accomplishments, pride in herself. He was making her feel whole.

How could this be wrong?

She wanted to break away, go back home, where she'd be

safe in her room, and meditate, ask for answers, figure out what to do.

But she was here, living her life instead of thinking about it, and she had to cope right now.

"Thank you for the picture, Jim. It's…it will always mean more to me than you can ever know."

"I'm glad." He stared at the photo with her while the silence grew charged between them. "What were you thinking about when I took the picture? Your face changed so dramatically."

"You." She answered automatically, then put the picture back in the folder. "I was thinking about you, Jim, and how much you've brought to my life in such a short time. I don't think I can ever—"

He stopped her sentence with a long, sweet kiss that shot her to the moon.

Somehow she managed to break away. "I can't do this."

"You *say* that. But everything you *do* tells me you feel very differently deep down."

"I need time to establish some independence and—"

His kiss that time was harder, more passionate, the type of kiss Tricia felt between her legs. "You think I'm going to ruin your independence?"

"It's not you, it's me. I become so dependent when I'm involved with someone. I've been so peaceful on my own, I've felt so strong. Around you I don't—" another kiss, longer that time "—feel peaceful."

"I don't feel peaceful around you, either, Tee." He picked her up, set her on the desk, stepped between her legs. "But I also think you're pushing me away based on some therapy theory, not on what's real. Being with the right person isn't damaging. Look at Melanie. Look at Alana."

"I don't…" She closed her eyes. She'd made so much sense to herself and now he was tearing it all apart. Melanie went from man to man, and was now with Edgar, partly because

Tricia had helped push her there. Why hadn't she told Melanie she should be single, whole on her own, powerful alone? Why did different rules apply to her?

"I want to kiss you again, Tricia. Hell, I want to do a lot more than that. I always have. But right now I'm being a good boy and asking permission, because I want you to want this as much as I do. Will you let me?"

She took in a deep breath, confusion and lust and need churning around, and then she thought of the picture, the woman she was in that picture, the woman she was with him. The woman she wanted to be.

"Yes."

He kissed her immediately, afraid she'd change her mind. She responded as if he were a drug she was still addicted to, wrapped her arms around him. *Jim.*

He kissed lower, on her jaw, down the side of her neck, gentle biting kisses that made shivers run over her skin.

Yes. Her inner voice finally spoke. Yes. Jim was nothing like her other men. Being with him was nothing like being with them. She felt none of the desperation, that if they didn't find her sexy and desirable over and over again, then she wasn't. She felt no shame for her middle-aged body. No worries that he'd find her flaws anything but enticing.

His mouth landed on hers again; she slid her hands around to his back, eased his shirt up and over his head. She loved the feel of his warm skin. She loved the scent and shape of his body.

Her skirt slid up her thighs while she unbuckled his pants. And when he slid inside her, emotion that wasn't gratitude swelled in her heart. She'd known him such a short time in her current incarnation. But she could swear that she was falling for him, had fallen for him. Maybe decades ago. Crazy. But nice. Maybe after she moved to Florida they could keep seeing each other. Slowly. Take it slowly, while she rekindled a relationship with her parents.

Yes.

Her inner voice spoke again. *Yes.*

She leaned back on the table, arching for him, so they could both watch him sliding in and out, the beautiful, remarkable, arousing sight.

"You're so beautiful."

She met his eyes then, without fear this time, and saw his growing feelings for her reflected in them. With him she felt beautiful. *Yes.*

But slowly. As slow and steady as his rhythm now, building and building until something really wonderful burst between them.

She caressed her breasts to make him crazy, then slid her hand down to touch herself, for him and for her. The climb in desire was immediate for them both; his rhythm accelerated, he breathed unevenly, harshly, pushing in and out, watching her fingers.

Her body told her she was ready. She moaned and clutched his shoulder. He got the signal, grabbed her hips and went harder, longer, until the orgasm swelled and exploded through her.

Yes. It was all going to be fine. She opened her eyes and saw him climax, his jaw clenching, his eyes closed in ecstasy.

Yes. This man was perfect. She could ease gradually back into a relationship, discover slowly what it was like to belong to—

"I love you, Tricia." He spoke gently, softly against her temple. "I've loved you for as long as I've known you. I wanted to kill Tom for leaving you, and then I wanted to take his place. It nearly broke me when you pulled away, but I waited. And then you left town, and I did break. For years. When I found out you were back, it was as if I could finally release a breath I'd been holding for all that time. Being with you is everything I've ever wanted."

"Jim..." She felt suspended between joy and fear. This didn't sound like slowly, and she desperately needed slowly. "I am... I mean I don't know what to say. Except that... Wow."

She cringed. What a completely inadequate response.

"No worries." He pulled out of her, eased her off the desk, held her close, rocked her gently. "I just needed to get all that out."

"You...took me by surprise."

"Nice surprise?"

She couldn't stand the vulnerability in his eyes. "Very nice. Very."

"So you think you could stand being in the same state with me down south?"

"What do you mean?" She forced herself not to tense in his arms.

"I had a move in mind before you came back. Beatrice mentioned it. I'm tired of winter. The cold and temperature changes give me migraines. I was thinking about living closer to Miami, more my scene down there, but Orlando is also a possibility."

"But..." She was stunned, thrilled, horrified.

"What, you don't want me near you?"

She laughed, pushed down her fears, put her arms around his neck. "I think I could stand it, yes."

"In the same town?"

"Sure." She laughed again, still uneasy, but still okay. He loved her. She was crazy about him. He'd be a rock on which she could get to steadier footing. And she was pretty sure before long she'd be in love with him, too, if she wasn't already, and could pay him back by being his rock in whatever way he needed.

"In the same house?"

"The same…" She blinked. Slowly. *Slo-o-w-ly.* "What are you saying? You want to live with me?"

"No." He dropped to one knee, took her hand and gazed up at her with adoration. "Tricia Hawthorne, I want to marry you."

17

MELANIE THUDDED downstairs, feeling as if her body had been replaced by cement blocks. She'd gotten home at 1:00 a.m., after her panicked dash away from poor Edgar's proposal, and hadn't slept much, if at all.

She needed coffee and a break from the panic and pain and excitement and guilt and God knew whatever else she was feeling. A whirling cesspool of emotions. No, wait, whirlpools whirled, cesspools didn't.

She needed a button she could press to turn off her thoughts while she took a break. Kind of like sleep mode for a computer.

Down in the kitchen, the coffeemaker was already going; her mom sat slumped over the counter, looking exactly the way Melanie felt.

"Morning." Melanie grabbed a mug and topped it up, wishing she could just mainline the caffeine into her veins. Wishing they made a substance in coffee that would not only perk her up, but organize her thoughts, too.

"Morning." Tricia's eyes were rimmed with red and swollen, her skin pale.

Uh-oh. "Um, how did things go with Jim last night?" She perched on a stool opposite her mother.

"Terrible. How did things go with Edgar last night?"

Melanie gulped coffee and groaned. "Terrible."

"You want to go first or should I?"

"You should, Mom." Melanie slumped on her stool. "My situation is pretty intense."

"Actually…" Her mother rubbed the center of her forehead as if it ached. "Mine is pretty out there, too."

"Really?" Melanie frowned. "Should we flip for it?"

Tricia managed a chuckle. "Tails I win, heads you lose?"

"I'll go first." She lifted her hand, volunteering, then that seemed too much effort so she let it smack down onto the counter. "Everything started out great. We drove down to Ravinia. He'd made a really nice picnic, and we lay out on the blanket and listened to the music. It was soothing to listen and to just relax together. I was feeling pretty crazy about him. No, really crazy about him. And then we came back here and everything was so great, and he ruined it."

Her mother made a tortured sound. "That sounds exactly like my evening. I mean about it being so intense and so fantastic and then boom, he ruined it."

"What did Jim do?"

"You won't believe it."

"Try me."

"He asked me to marry him." Tricia shook her head as if she couldn't imagine anything more horrible.

Melanie's jaw dropped. "You're kidding."

"I know, isn't it unbelievable?" Her mom had flushed; she was looking extremely agitated. "I mean we barely know each other, or haven't for years and years. No, decades. He can't possible think marriage is a sensible or practical or in any way good idea. Plus now he's threatening to move to Florida with me."

Melanie cringed. "He's changing his entire life after seeing you *twice?*"

"I know. I know." Tricia opened her tired eyes wider. "I couldn't get away fast enough."

"I don't blame you." Melanie tsk-tsked, shaking her head. "No relationship can survive that kind of pressure."

"Exactly what I think." She tapped the counter smartly for emphasis. "Exactly."

"That's because you're right."

"I know I am." She didn't look at all happy to be right, but stared dully into her cup.

Melanie thought that sounded like a good idea, so she stared dully into hers, too, wishing she could think of the perfect comforting thing to say to her mother. A tiny part of her did think Jim was pretty passionate and romantic, asking Mom to marry him so soon. He must be so sure. She couldn't imagine.

"What did Edgar do to screw up your evening?"

Melanie sighed and dropped her head, letting her hair tumble over her face. "You really will not believe this."

"Try me."

"He asked me to marry him." She lifted her face to get Mom's reaction.

Tricia's jaw took its turn to drop. "You are *kidding*."

"Nope."

"My God, that's statistically impossible. Same night? Same family?"

"I know." Melanie sighed glumly, but she couldn't quell the excitement darting around inside her.

"What did you do?"

"Same as you. I freaked out and bolted." She sighed. "Poor Edgar."

Her mother sighed. "Poor Jim."

A sharp knock at the back door made them both jump, then jump again when the door burst open. Alana stood, grinning, putting her house key back in her pocket. "Good morning! Beautiful morning!"

Melanie and her mom exchanged glances. "Hi, Alana."

"How is everyone on this glorious summer day?" Alana looked from one pale exhausted face to the other. "Uh...did anyone get any sleep last night?"

"Not much."

"Me neither." She giggled and started fluttering her fingers. "Me neither. Notice anything?"

Melanie stared. "Other than you looking disgustingly perky?"

"And waggling around for some reason?"

Alana put her hands up and patted the sides of her face. "Anything now? Anything?"

"New makeup?" Tricia asked.

"Cosmetic surgery?" Melanie was so not in the mood to play guessing games.

"You are both hopeless. This!" Alana pointed energetically to the ring on the fourth finger of her left hand, which didn't stand out immediately because of the rings on her other fingers. "Sawyer asked me to marry him last night after dinner at Sanford's!"

She stood expectantly, beaming broadly.

Trish's mug hit the table. "Oh. My—"

"God," Melanie finished for her.

"What?" Irritation and hurt polluted Alana's elation. "I thought you'd be pleased."

"We *are*." Melanie got up, horribly ashamed of her reaction, trying to make her voice as hearty as possible. "I'm sorry. We're really pleased. Sawyer is a fabulous guy. I know you guys will be *so*, so happy, sweetie. Congratulations."

"What is going on, Mel?" She turned to Tricia in the middle of Melanie's attempt at hugging her. "Mom? You both look miserable."

"Don't worry about that." Melanie forced a smile and patted her sister's back. "Isn't the ring magnificent, Mom?"

"It is." Tricia nodded rapidly, as if she were trying to shake her head loose. "Sweetie, I'm thrilled. And so happy to be here when this happened to you—er, happened for you."

"Okay." Alana actually let Mom hug her, then scowled and folded her arms across her chest. "I want to know immediately what is bothering both of you or I'm not going to enjoy the rest of this day at all and that will be entirely your fault and on your heads for the rest of your lives."

Silence. Melanie looked at her mom. Her mom looked at her.

"Well…" Melanie started. "The timing is…interesting, that's all?"

"Why?"

"Edgar asked Melanie to marry him last night," Tricia said.

"Melanie!" Alana's eyes lit up again. "That is so—"

"And Jim asked Mom to marry him last night."

"—amazing." Alana's joy turned cautious. "Wow. Um. Wow."

"Yeah, wow." Melanie stared back into her coffee.

"Amazing." Tricia sighed.

Alana's scowl returned. "I take it there are no congratulations to hand around."

Tricia shook her head.

"Um…no." Melanie couldn't look at her sister. Seeing this through her eyes made the whole thing look very different.

"So, you turned them down, which was what you wanted." Alana jammed her hands on her hips. "And now, as a result of this brilliant bit of decision making, the two of you are absolutely miserable."

"I guess we are," Tricia said miserably.

"Yup," said Melanie, equally miserably.

"Well, pardon me for being direct, but it seems to me if you'd made the right decisions, you'd both be relieved and happy."

"Oh." Melanie rubbed her nose. "It's more complicated than that."

"No, it isn't." Alana used her best know-it-all voice.

"Really." Melanie started to bristle.

"I'll put it simply. In fact, I'll quote you, Melanie, from a few weeks ago, when I was still stupidly resisting commitment to Sawyer." She started flapping chicken arms. *"Buk-buk-buk, buk-eek."*

"Stop that."

Alana sighed and drew up a stool next to Melanie, clasped her hands so the brilliant diamond on her finger sparkled unavoidably.

"Okay. Talk to me. Mom, why did you say no?"

"I told him…that I wanted to be whole on my own and not be dependent on a man again for my happiness."

Melanie frowned. "But you haven't dated for a year. And it sounds like Jim cares about your happiness more than you do."

Tricia shifted uncomfortably. "He's more grounded than the other men I've been with, but that doesn't mean much, frankly."

Melanie turned to Alana, not as sure as she was earlier that her mother was smart to escape. "He's offering to move to Florida to be with her."

Alana threw up a hand in frustration. "Changing his whole life so he doesn't have to lose you? Do you have any idea how remarkable that is? Have any of the guys you've been with before offered to change so much as a hairstyle for you?"

"No." Tricia bowed her head meekly, and it occurred to Melanie that the mom-daughter roles were once more reversed in their family. And maybe that was just how it was going to be sometimes, and maybe not something that had to be changed anymore.

"I didn't think so. And hey, Edgar can buy Jim's studio building if he moves. It's perfect for both of them."

Tricia and Melanie gazed at her mournfully.

"Honestly." Alana jabbed her finger at Melanie. "Your turn."

"Uh-oh."

"What did you say to poor Edgar?"

"That he was moving way too fast, that we were barely getting to know each other and—"

"You've known him two years. Adored him for two years. How many other men have you treasured that much even for two weeks? More importantly, how many of them have hung around even half that long?"

"Um." She fidgeted with her coffee. "None."

"And how many men do you think you'll meet in this world who fit you and tolerate you and adore you the way he does?" Her voice softened. "That's how Sawyer makes me feel. Like the most amazing woman ever produced on this earth. Like even my worst most horrible PMS days won't scare him away because he knows I'm still in there somewhere. Do you know how rare that is?"

Melanie hung her head. "Yes, Mommy. No, Mommy."

Silence. Tricia snorted.

Alana snorted, too, sounding exactly the same as her mother. And then they were all laughing together, maybe a little maniacally, but it was still music to Melanie's ears.

More than that, while she was laughing with her mother and her sister, Alana's words were percolating in her brain. He adored her. She adored him. He challenged her mind, challenged her to be a better person, made her sizzle with passion. She could tell him anything. He was her closest, most constant friend. He'd seen her at her worst, accepted every part of her and loved her still.

What more did she want in her life and in her heart? Why was she letting fear get between herself and what she'd always dreamed of?

The rest of the day she spent in a numb daze, caught in the

battle between logic and fear. She should call Edgar. Maybe she just needed more time. Maybe...

Maybe she *was* just being chicken.

She and her mother took Alana and Sawyer out to celebrate their engagement. Seeing the two of them so happy...well, Melanie wasn't the only one throwing wistful looks their way. Tricia was practically salivating.

Finally, after dessert and coffee, Melanie got restless from lovey-dovey overload and got up to go to the bathroom. Tricia went with her.

"I can't stand this anymore." Melanie stood at the sink washing her hands. "I want what they have. No, that's not even true. I *have* what they have. I've just been too scared and silly to enjoy it."

Tricia met her eyes in the mirror, looking strained and anxious. "So what are you going to do?"

"I'm going over to Edgar's after dinner." She dried her hands and threw the towel away. "And I think you should go over to Jim's."

"No. No, I couldn't do that." The denial sounded automatic. Her mother's eyes were lit with excitement. "We've only been on two dates. You and Edgar have known each other for years."

"You've known him twenty-five years."

"I've changed."

"I have, too. But I think who we are at our core hasn't changed. Both of us were looking for love, Mom. We were just going about it the wrong way. Now we've found it, we can't turn and run. It would make a complete mockery of everything we've come to understand about ourselves and our feelings. If you don't want to marry him yet, don't. But don't lose him, either. Go tonight. We can meet for breakfast and see how it went."

"I...don't—"

Melanie put her hands to her shoulders, started flapping. "*Buk-buk-buk, buk*-eek."

Tricia laughed and drew her in for a long hug. Melanie buried her head in her mom's shoulder. Her life was coming together, finally. Family and love. Marriage and children with Edgar. Children she could be a solid, steady mom to, stay home at night—most nights—and bake cookies, join the PTA, drive them to soccer....

Someday.

Right now, tonight, she had something *much* more fun in mind.

EDGAR LAY IN BED. He wasn't sleepy; it was only eleven, but he hadn't been able to keep his mind on books or TV, didn't want to practice fencing, the kitchen didn't appeal, neither did bars or movies or concerts—in short, he was in a prime, grade A funk. To make it worse, Kaitlin and Stoner had come over before going out again—he hoped soon—and were laughing and being revoltingly goopy in the living room, something he didn't think his brother would stoop to, but that's what love did. Edgar would rather do just about anything than have to be around that, so he figured if he was going to be brooding and miserable, he might as well do it in his room, in bed, in the dark, so he could be truly and outstandingly pathetic.

Stoner mumbled something in the next room, which made Kaitlin giggle. Edgar drew the sheet over his head. Maybe he had earplugs somewhere, but theoretically Goopy and Giggles were leaving soon, and anyway, he didn't have the energy even to remember where the earplugs were.

A knock on the door; Stoner answering. Probably one of the friends they were meeting for a night of dancing and drinking and titillation and fun before they crashed at Kaitlin's house and got to screw each other's brains out all night long. Kaitlin had already quit her job at Caffe Coffee and signed on as the band's PR director, revamping their Web site, working on getting a buzz to go viral online. When she graduated from Marquette in December, she'd be traveling with the band, and most likely whip them all into shape. Edgar was glad for Stoner. When love hit like that…

He groaned and turned over, his face pressed into his pillow until his need for air overcame his need to punish himself. What now? For him, what now? See if he could salvage something from the horrible mistake he'd made with Melanie? Leave her alone to calm down and think over how she felt? He didn't know. Maybe he'd misread her. Maybe he was a hopeless romantic thinking his love could be enough to cure her restless searching in all the wrong places. Maybe she really was too damaged by her upbringing and experiences with her mother to let herself commit to one man. Maybe in ten years she would, maybe twenty—he couldn't put his life on hold that long to find out.

If nothing else, she'd given him a lot. More confidence in himself and the value of what he had to offer women. He'd have that for the rest of his life even if he didn't have her.

He groaned again. It was the part about not having her that he wasn't sure he could survive.

His bedroom door opened. He stiffened. What the hell? Had Stoner left something in here?

"What's going on?"

"Shhh." The door illuminated a silhouette for a brief second before it closed.

He knew that silhouette. Knew it inside out. He even knew that "Shhh." His heart started pounding. Melanie wouldn't come all the way over here tonight to reject him again. Had she changed her mind? About marrying him? He didn't care. She was here.

"Kaitlin!" He pretended annoyance. "If you want something, just say so."

"Yeah, I want something," she whispered. He heard the sound of clothes being taken off, hitting the floor.

"Again?" He grinned, his cock stirring immediately. "Look, kid, I can have sex only so many times a day."

Silence. No more clothes noises. "You—"

"Melanie." He threw back the sheet. "Get in bed."

"Why you—" She hurled herself in with him, wrapped her body around his. "I thought—"

"Never." He kissed her, touched her everywhere. "I know you, Melanie. You could call me on a terrible connection from the middle of Antarctica in the middle of the night, not say a word, and I'd recognize you from your breathing."

She laughed softly. "In that case you're a complete pig to put me through that, even for a second."

"I'm sorry." He stroked her hair, tried to stop himself from hauling out bondage materials and tying her to his bed so she'd never leave again.

"No." She put a finger to his lips. "*I'm* sorry. Sorry I freaked out so badly last night. I really do love you, Edgar."

Oh, thank you, God. He could get down on his knees and be grateful the rest of his life and it still wouldn't be enough. "I love you, too, Mel."

She kissed him, drew her tongue across his lips, kissed him again. He tried very hard to stay sweet and supportive, but she was in bed with him, wearing only underpants, which was driving him completely insane. She felt so good. She smelled so good. She *was* so good.

And maybe now, *finally,* now, she'd really be his.

"It was my fault." He stroked her, up and down, stopping demurely at the small of her back. "The last thing to do to someone recovering from commitment phobia is demand commitment before she's ready."

"I am ready." She wrapped her legs around his hips, started a gentle pulsing rhythm against one of his favorite parts. "Mmm, getting readier all the time."

"You are?" He took charge of the rhythm, dipped his hands under the elastic of her panties. Was she talking about—

"Yes, Edgar," she whispered.

He had to be sure. "Are we talking about sex or commitment?"

"Keep doing that and you'll find out."

He groaned and untangled their legs, yanked down her panties and made her writhe to the point of gasping with his tongue, then he grabbed a condom and rolled over her, pinioned her wrists over her head and looked into her beautiful blue eyes, darkened from desire. For him. Plain old Edgar. "Let me ask you again. Are you ready?"

"Yes-s-s."

He slid inside her; they rocked together, feverishly, impatiently, greedy for each other, familiar but also new tonight, a beginning.

She held his shoulders, turned to whisper in his ear. "Ask me again."

"If you're ready?"

"To marry you."

He lifted, looked down into her adored face and felt the rest of his life's happiness contained in this one awesome, humbling moment.

"Melanie, my incredibly beautiful and sexually arousing love, will you marry me?"

She giggled, brought his head down for a long sweet kiss, then met his eyes, hers honest and clear of doubts. "Yes, Edgar. I will marry you. Because of all my sexy and exciting bad boys, you're the most sexy and the most exciting. And the only one I'll need for the rest of my life."

Epilogue

Society Page, Milwaukee Tribune, December 22

ALANA HAWTHORNE WAS married to Sawyer Kern last Saturday in a moving ceremony at Church of the Gesu in Milwaukee. The weather cooperated, providing a chilly but brilliantly sunny day—the predicted snowstorm passed to the south. Sources close to the bride revealed that she'd been performing antisnow dances with Mr. Kern's nephews all week long.

Ms. Hawthorne wore a stunningly elegant strapless embroidered lace sheath gown, adorned with beads and sequins, that emphasized her slender height and dark beauty. She was accompanied down the aisle to the strains of a Mozart quartet by her soon-to-be stepfather, Jim Bronson, who presented her to her groom beaming with pride. The entire Kern family and the cream of Milwaukee's fine citizens were arranged throughout the spacious church, the nave of which was nearly full.

Mr. and Mrs. Sawyer Kern celebrated their marriage immediately afterward at the exclusive University Club of Milwaukee with lobster, filet mignon and champagne. The newlyweds took time off from their work at the Kern Family Foundation supporting local artists to honeymoon in St. Thomas.

Harley Museum Newsletter, June

On May 8 we hosted the marriage of Jim Bronson and Tricia Hawthorne outdoors on our grounds by the Menomonee River on an overcast but *warm* day—unusual for spring in Milwaukee, right? The bride looked beautiful in a cream-colored linen suit, the groom dapper in jeans and a black leather vest.

After witnessing the happy couple's vows, the few dozen family members and close friends feasted on Solly's butter burgers and Usinger brats washed down with Wisconsin beer. The "cake" was an enormous mountain of cream puffs, the annual Wisconsin State Fair favorite. Music was provided by the fabulous Paul Cebar and his band Tomorrow Sound, and all passersby were encouraged to join in the dancing, which they did in droves.

The couple purred off on Jim's vintage Electra Glide bike to honeymoon on the shores of Lake Michigan in northern Wisconsin's Door County. Jim and Tricia plan to move to Florida at the end of the month, where Jim will establish a new photography studio and Ms. Hawthorne will launch a career as a children's book author and illustrator. Her first work, *The Calendar Witch*, will be published by Kent Press next June.

Letter postmarked June 30, Santa Fe, NM

DEAR FAMILY AND FRIENDS,

Yesterday Edgar and I had the best day of our lives. First, he won a bronze medal in the fencing match! While he was standing on the podium I thought I'd explode with pride. To celebrate we went out on the town—yes, I even got him dancing. That was last night.

This morning…brace yourselves. We're married! It was so beautiful. We got the license yesterday and then by some incredible chance, there was an opening at the magistrate court today, and we jumped on it. I know you all wanted to be there, I'm sorry for that, but when we arrived here, we realized we just couldn't wait any longer (no, Alana, I'm not pregnant). He is everything I've ever wanted—thank God I grew up enough to realize that—and it's more and more miraculous to me every day that he thinks I'm as wonderful as he does.

I promise we'll have a second ceremony in Milwaukee or maybe just a party when we get back, but for now we are Mr. and Mrs. Edgar Raymond! I've never been more sure I've done the right thing and I've never, *ever* been happier.

Sending love, see you next week!

Melanie

Harlequin offers a romance for every mood!
See below for a sneak peek
from our suspense romance line
Silhouette® Romantic Suspense.
Introducing HER HERO IN HIDING by
New York Times *bestselling author Rachel Lee.*

Kay Young returned to woozy consciousness to find that she was lying on a soft sofa beneath a heap of quilts near a cheerfully burning fire. When she tried to move, however, everything hurt, and she groaned.

At once she heard a sound, then a stranger with a hard, harsh face was squatting beside her. "Shh," he said softly. "You're safe here. I promise."

"I have to go," she said weakly, struggling against pain. "He'll find me. He can't find me."

"Easy, lady," he said quietly. "You're hurt. No one's going to find you here."

"He will," she said desperately, terror clutching at her insides. "He always finds me!"

"Easy," he said again. "There's a blizzard outside. No one's getting here tonight, not even the doctor. I know, because I tried."

"Doctor? I don't need a doctor! I've got to get away."

"There's nowhere to go tonight," he said levelly. "And if I thought you could stand, I'd take you to a window and show you."

But even as she tried once more to pull away the quilts, she remembered something else: this man had been gentle when he'd found her beside the road, even when she had kicked and clawed. He hadn't hurt her.

Terror receded just a bit. She looked at him and detected signs of true concern there.

The terror eased another notch and she let her head sag on the pillow. "He always finds me," she whispered.

"Not here. Not tonight. That much I can guarantee."

*Will Kay's mysterious rescuer protect her
from her worst fears?
Find out in HER HERO IN HIDING by New York Times
bestselling author Rachel Lee.
Available June 2010, only from
Silhouette® Romantic Suspense.*